The steps were approaching Aunt Margaret's door now. Perhaps she heard them and was too frightened to cry out. Sarah thought about what that would be like — to lie helpless in bed, unable to move, waiting, waiting....

"Somebody! Help me!" Aunt Margaret cried out. With a gasp, Sarah raced up the stairs. She ran across the room to where her great-aunt huddled under the comforter. Her blue eyes were glazed with terror.

"Who is it?" she cried. "Who's out there?"

Sarah looked over her shoulder. The doorway was empty. "I — I don't know," she stammered.

A Ghost in the House

Betty Ren Wright

AN
APPLE
PAPERBACK

SCHOLASTIC INC.
New York Toronto London Auckland Sydney

No part of this publication may be reproduced in whole or in part, or stored in a retrieval system, or transmitted in any form or by any means, electronic, mechanical, photocopying, recording, or otherwise, without written permission of the publisher. For information regarding permission, write to Scholastic Inc., 730 Broadway, New York, NY 10003.

ISBN 0-590-43603-1

12 11 10 9 8 7 6 5 4 3 2   3 4 5 6 7/9

Printed in the U.S.A.   40

For my mother

A Ghost in the House

One

I DON'T JUST *like* this room," Sarah Prescott exclaimed. "I *like* basketball and peanut-brittle ice cream and scary movies. I *love* this room. I love the window seat and the fireplace and everything else."

"I know," Lutie Marks said, but of course she didn't. Even though she was Sarah's best friend, she couldn't know how important this bedroom was. Lutie had had her own bedroom all her life. She'd never had to share her space with a little brother. Lutie had grown up here in suburban Willow Park, with trees and grass and flowers outside her windows in the summer, and a furnace that was big enough to keep her whole house warm in the winter. She took these wonders for granted. Sarah had been enjoying them for only six months, since her father had found his good-paying dream job at the electronics plant, and they had moved from Milwaukee's crowded inner city.

"I said I liked it, too." Lutie sounded a little annoyed. "It's perfect just the way it is. I don't see why you want a different picture over the fireplace."

The girls were sitting side by side on the edge of the four-poster bed, looking at the painting they'd just carried in from the storeroom and propped against the wall. "It's pretty," Lutie admitted. "That path through the woods is sort of mysterious, and I like the way the sunlight comes through the leaves. But the portrait looks as if it belongs up there right where it is. Why take it down?"

Sarah narrowed her eyes at the smiling girl in the painting. Lutie had put her finger on the problem without knowing it. Once, long ago, this bedroom had belonged to that girl. *But not any more,* Sarah thought fiercely. *It's my room now.*

She knew it was silly to be jealous of a girl in a painting, especially when that girl was now a sick old lady in a nursing home. *But I'm not really jealous,* Sarah told herself. *I just don't want to be reminded that this wasn't always our house.*

"That girl even looks like you," Lutie persisted. "You both have straight brown hair and blue eyes—and look! She has the same little dimple in her chin that you have. Is she related to you?"

"She's my dad's aunt," Sarah said. "She grew up in this house, and then she moved to Washington and taught school there for forty years. Her folks lived here till they were very old, and after that the house was rented to relatives and to other people who kept it pretty much the way it was—the furniture and everything. Aunt Margaret always thought she'd come back here to Milwaukee after she retired, but when she finally did come back she had to go to a nursing home instead." Sarah raced through the history impatiently. None of it mattered. Even though she and her family were only renting the house, she felt as if it belonged to *them*. She felt as if her life—her *real* life—had begun on the shining June day when they moved in.

"If I had a painting of an ancestor, I'd keep it up on the wall for everybody to see," Lutie said earnestly. "Especially if the ancestor looked like me. And especially if she was thin."

Thinness was important to Lutie. Every day she leaned into the rest-room mirror at school, hoping to find cheekbones in her round, rosy face.

"Well, I don't have to decide right now," Sarah said. Perhaps Lutie was right. Maybe having her great-aunt's portrait over the fireplace made the bedroom more Sarah's own, not less. She'd have to think about it. "Come on, let's go downstairs and get some gingersnaps. My mother's been baking."

"I know." Lutie sniffed hungrily. "Your house always smells terrific. I wish my mother liked to bake." She followed Sarah out to the upper hall and down the wide staircase.

"My mom didn't always do it," Sarah said. "She likes the kitchen in this house because it's big and sunny and fun to work in." Sarah thought of the other kitchens she'd known before this one. There had been a whole series of them, as her father moved from job to job—tiny, dark, crowded kitchens in small, dreary flats and apartments. They were places where you cooked meals, washed dishes, and from which you escaped as quickly as possible. Lutie had probably never been in a kitchen like that.

Sarah's little brother Lloyd was sitting at the round kitchen table reading a comic book and gobbling cookies. Gabe, the black Labrador, lay at his feet with one eye open, watching for crumbs.

"*The Thing from the Tomb.*" Sarah peered over his shoulder as she slid into a chair. "Yuk! How can you read that stuff? I'd have nightmares."

"You're a girl," Lloyd muttered without looking up. "You're scared of everything."

Sarah rolled her eyes and pushed the plate of cookies toward Lutie.

"Girls are braver than boys," she said automatically. "They're braver, smarter, and stronger. And they live longer. Who's Mom talking to on the phone?" she hurried on. "She sounds sort of grim."

Lloyd shrugged. "Mrs. Somebody. They've been talking for a real long time. I heard her say she'd discuss it—whatever *it* is—with the family tonight." He looked up with a wicked little grin. "It might be one of your teachers," he said slyly. "Maybe you're flunking jography."

"Ge-og-ra-phy," Sarah said. "And it's not one of my teachers," She knew she'd been doing well in all her classes at Pioneer Middle School.

"Maybe your mother is talking to my mother about the Cavemen concert," Lutie suggested. "Have you asked if you can go?"

"We talked about it, and they didn't say no. My dad said thirty-five dollars is too much for a concert, but he doesn't like rock music in the first place. He'll go along if my mother says it's okay. I think maybe they'll call it a Christmas present."

"Great." Lutie beamed. "And did you ask if we can have the sleepover here after the concert?"

"Not yet," Sarah replied. "But I know it'll be okay."

That was another wonderful thing about living in a big house in the suburbs. There was room for friends to stay overnight. Twice since school started this fall, some of Sarah's classmates had brought their bedrolls and "camped out" in front of the fireplace in her bedroom. They had popped corn over the fire and told ghost stories, and everyone said they were the best sleepovers they'd ever had.

Lutie glanced at her watch and jumped up. "If that *is* my mother on the phone, tell her I'm on my way," she said hastily. "I'm supposed to be at the dentist's office at four-thirty." She ignored Lloyd who leaned back in his chair, mouth wide open, and squirmed in make-believe agony. "Call me tonight and tell me what you're going to do about the painting," she suggested. "If you don't want the portrait, maybe your folks will let you lend her to me. She can be *my* ancestor for a while."

Sarah walked with her friend to the front door and lingered there, listening to her mother's conversation in the little "telephone room" under the stairs. The person on the other end of the line was doing most of the talking, but there was something in Mrs. Prescott's soft "I see—well, we'll have to discuss it" that made Sarah uneasy. Life was so perfect now; she couldn't bear to think anything might be wrong.

Bracing herself, she went back down the hall just as her mother was saying good-bye.

"Well." Mrs. Prescott drew a deep breath and shook her head as if to clear it. "Every day brings its surprises."

"What surprises?" Sarah demanded. "Who were you talking to?"

"The social worker at Aunt Margaret's nursing home," Mrs. Prescott said. "There were some things she wanted to discuss."

A wave of relief washed over Sarah. She didn't know what she'd been afraid of, but she could stop worrying now. Whatever was happening at Menlo Manor Nursing Home, it could have little to do with Sarah Prescott's world.

"Is Aunt Margaret feeling worse?"

Sarah's mother looked at her thoughtfully for a moment before she replied. "No," she said. "As a matter of fact, she's quite a bit stronger than she was the last time we were there. The therapy seems to be helping her arthritis." She stood up and stretched. "We'll talk about it tonight when your father gets home from work," she said. "Right now I'd better get back to the kitchen and rescue those cookies before Lloyd eats them all."

An hour later Sarah had finished her weekend homework and had made up her mind about the painting. The portrait would come down, and the forest would go up in its place. The woodland scene brought back great memories of the camping trip she and her family had taken two years before. They had borrowed a tent and cooked all their meals over an open fire, and Sarah and Lloyd had enjoyed every minute of it. They had hiked on paths like the one in the painting and had tried to identify the birds chattering overhead. The painting reminded Sarah of a good time she hoped to repeat someday and, after all, the girl in the portrait didn't even exist anymore. In her place was an old lady whom Sarah had visited a few times but hardly knew.

That question settled, she stretched out on her bed and tried to think of ways to convince her parents that she *must* go to the Cavemen concert. A car turned into the driveway, tires scrunching over the snow-covered gravel. Snow made her think of ice, and ice reminded her of skating. Maybe she and Lutie could go ice-skating the next day. The pond, a block away, was supposed to be ready for skaters this weekend if the cold weather held.

She stretched lazily, then frowned. Whoever had driven in was taking a long time to get out of the car. Downstairs, Gabe barked impatiently. Sarah glanced at her watch and saw that it was only four-thirty—much too early for her father to come home.

She got up and knelt on the window seat. It *was* her father's car. She could see him at the wheel, just sitting there, looking straight ahead, as if he hadn't noticed he was in his own backyard.

She watched, puzzled, until the car door finally opened and her father stepped out. He was wearing the bright red earmuffs she'd given him for Christmas last year, and his longish brown hair blew in the wind. He walked slowly across the snow to the house—so slowly that Sarah was waiting downstairs in the kitchen by the time he opened the door. Her mother and Lloyd were there, too.

"Hi, hon, you're home early. How was your day?" Mrs. Prescott's voice was cheerful, but her eyes were worried. Lloyd had pushed aside *The Thing from the Tomb* to stare at his father.

Mr. Prescott tried to smile. He sat down heavily in a kitchen chair and began unwinding his red woolen scarf. Gabe leaned against his knee.

"My day was not so good. It wasn't good at all. We got called into a meeting after lunch. They're closing the whole plant—transferring the work to another location out East. I'm through."

"Oh, no!" Sarah's mother stepped backward, as if she'd been struck. "They couldn't do that to you, not after just six months. I thought the business was going so well."

"It is," Mr. Prescott said tiredly. "And it will be even better if the whole company's under one roof. At least," he added, "that's what their accountants tell them."

Sarah's head whirled. "It's not true!" she cried. "You can't be out of work—not again!" There had to be some mistake. Her father must have misunderstood what was going to happen.

"Sarah, be still!" Mrs. Prescott sounded furious. "Can't you see what a blow this is for your father?"

But Sarah couldn't stop. "You can't be fired," she shouted. "You just can't, Daddy. That's stupid!"

Mrs. Prescott gasped. "Sarah," she snapped. "Go to your room. Now!"

Sarah turned and ran down the hall. Halfway up the stairs she stopped and leaned over the bannister. "I don't care," she sobbed. "I'm not going to move out of this house—not ever. You can't make me!"

But even as she said it, she knew the terrible truth. Without the job at the electronics plant, they couldn't afford the rent for the house—twice as much as any house they'd ever lived in before.

The perfect life was over.

Two

"COME ON, EVERYBODY, you have to eat." Mrs. Prescott looked down at her own practically untouched plate. "This isn't the end of the world, you know."

"Feels like it is," Mr. Prescott said. "I guess you'd better put my dinner in the refrigerator, and I'll warm it up later if I get hungry."

"I'll eat your mashed potatoes, if you don't want 'em," Lloyd offered generously. "You wouldn't want warmed-up mashed potatoes, would you?"

Sarah looked at her little brother in disgust. If the world were ending, he'd still want to eat. She'd given up on her own juicy, brown pork chop after one bite; it tasted like cardboard.

Mrs. Prescott sighed. "You might as well pick up the plates, Sarah," she said. "Then come back in here and sit down. We have some talking to do."

Eyes downcast, Sarah began gathering up dishes and carrying them to the kitchen. Usually they had their evening meal there, but tonight her mother had set the table in the dining room. It was a pretty room, with rich dark paneling topped by faded-but-nice wallpaper. Electric candles made pink haloes of light against the walls. It was a room that could make almost any meal festive, but tonight the magic hadn't worked. Sarah wondered how many more times they would sit there together.

She came back from the kitchen and slumped into her chair. "How soon do we have to move?" she asked. "You might as well tell us."

Her father sipped his coffee. "Let's try to think about this a little more positively," he suggested mildly. "After all, I may find something else right away."

"Maybe not," Sarah persisted. She was too miserable to notice how her father winced at her icy tone. "You said yourself this job was a miracle, Dad. Most companies want a college degree, no matter how much you know about electronics. I don't see how you think—"

"Sarah," Mrs. Prescott spoke warningly.

Sarah's father put up a hand. "Might as well speak frankly. And Sarah's right in a way—it will be pretty astounding if I find another job as good as this one was. But I'll certainly try. And in the meantime," he forced a smile, "we all have to stick together. Sarah, we aren't going to starve. Your mother is getting lots of typing jobs from the instructors and students at the college. And I'll find a temporary job to help us get by while I'm looking for something better. We'll manage."

Sarah bit her lip. She wasn't worrying about starving, and her father knew it. Her parents just didn't understand how much this house meant to her. Leaving it would break her heart.

She pushed back her chair and stood up. "I'm going to call Lutie," she said. "Might as well tell her the bad news."

"You're going to sit down," Mrs. Prescott said sharply. "Stop playing the martyr, Sarah. This isn't happening just to you, it's happening to all of us. And I have something to tell you that might make a difference."

Sarah sat.

"We're going to have to find new ways of earning money—or cutting expenses," her mother continued. "All agreed?"

"I have an idea," Lloyd announced. "Lots of kids at school think this house is haunted. We can have tours, and make people pay to look around. And I can hide in a closet and jump out at them, and we can make up stories about weird noises in the attic and—"

"That's silly," Sarah said. "This house is not

haunted. Just because it's old and big—"

"Stop it, you two." Mrs. Prescott reached over and tousled Lloyd's thatch of brown curls. "I don't think your idea will work, dear, but I'm glad you're looking for ways to help." Her glance flicked over Sarah, and then she continued. "I had a call this afternoon from Mrs. Ackerman, the social worker at Aunt Margaret's nursing home. She wanted to tell me that Margaret is gaining strength. She's still in a wheelchair, but the therapy she's been having has helped a lot."

"Hey, that's wonderful!" For the first time since he'd come home, Mr. Prescott's smile looked real. "I'm happy for her."

Sarah waited. She was happy for Aunt Margaret, too, but she didn't see why they were talking about her now. The house was what mattered, and how they were going to pay the rent.

"In fact," Mrs. Prescott went on, "she's so much better that her doctor thinks it would be possible for her to leave Menlo Manor and live at home. If she had a home, that is, and a family to take care of her." She paused.

"You mean she could come *here*?" Mr. Prescott sounded excited.

"Actually, it's Mrs. Ackerman's idea," Sarah's mother said. "She hasn't even mentioned the possibility to anyone else. But she says Margaret has talked a great deal about how she had always hoped to live here again, in her old age. She remembers every corner of the house, apparently. Mrs. Ackerman thought she'd just present the idea to us, and if we say no that'll be the end of it."

"It would be a lot of work," Mr. Prescott said. "Especially for you, Ruth. Aunt Margaret may be better than she was, but I'll bet she's still going to need lots of nursing. Could you do it?"

"I think so," Mrs. Prescott replied cautiously, "if all of you pitched in and helped."

Sarah looked from one of her parents to the other. What was going on here? Suddenly she thought she understood.

"Would Aunt Margaret pay to live with us?" she asked. "Is that what you meant about earning extra money?"

"Sarah, this house *belongs* to Aunt Margaret," Mrs. Prescott said. "She doesn't have a big income—that's why she has to charge us a fairly high rent. But if she could leave that expensive nursing home and stay with us, I'm sure we could work out some kind of financial arrangement. If we offered her a good home and lots of loving care, I doubt she'd want us to pay any rent at all."

Sarah had always wondered what a person meant when she said her heart jumped with joy. Now she knew. There was a wonderful *thud* in her chest that lifted her right out of her chair. Gabe, who had been lying at her feet, leapt up, too.

"But that's—that's super!" she gasped. "Why didn't you tell us before, Mom? It solves the whole problem!"

"Haunted house tours would be more fun," Lloyd said. He bared his teeth at Sarah and crossed his eyes. "I could be the Thing from the Tomb."

"Call the nursing home right away," Sarah begged her mother. "Tell them Aunt Margaret can come here. Please!"

Mrs. Prescott shook her head. "This is something to think about calmly," she said. "Taking care of an elderly invalid is a big job. I'm willing to try, but it will mean you and Lloyd will have to do a lot of chores around the house. And there will be other sacrifices as well."

Sarah hesitated. Her mother was watching her intently. "I don't mind doing chores," Sarah said. "What 'other sacrifices' do you mean?"

"Where would Aunt Margaret sleep?" Sarah's father asked abruptly. "The house is big, but the only spare space is that storeroom at the end of the hall. I don't think you could maneuver a wheelchair in there."

Mrs. Prescott nodded, her eyes still on Sarah. "Mrs. Ackerman says Margaret has talked frequently about the room she had when she was a girl. It had a fireplace and sloping ceilings and—well, you know what it's like."

"Uh-oh." Lloyd turned to stare at his sister.

"That's *my* room," Sarah said, suddenly

numbed. "You want to give Aunt Margaret my bedroom!"

"*Her* bedroom," Mrs. Prescott correctly gently. "And if it turns out that Aunt Margaret makes it possible for us to go on living here—enjoying this house and the garden and your schools and your new friends—well, then, I think the least we can do is let her have the room she remembers and loves so much."

Sarah shrank back in her chair. They were all watching her now, waiting. Sarah's mother looked expectant, and her father looked depressed. For once, Lloyd didn't try to make a joke.

"It's not fair," Sarah said finally. "It's the nicest bedroom I've ever had, and now you want me to say I wouldn't mind moving out so *she* can move in. You don't care how I feel."

"We're not asking you to do anything," Mrs. Prescott said. "I'm just trying to make it clear what will be involved if we say yes to Mrs. Ackerman. Aunt Margaret mustn't think for one minute that we're taking her in grudgingly."

"I wish I could promise we could stay here whether she comes or not," Sarah's father said apologetically. "I know this is hard on you, Sarah. Still—"

"We don't have to make any decisions right now." Mrs. Prescott reached across the table and squeezed Sarah's hand. "I told Mrs. Ackerman I'd call her back Monday morning, so we have plenty of time to think about it."

Sarah nodded. She would think about it, all right. How could she think about anything else? But she knew already that only one decision was possible. They would invite Aunt Margaret to come and live with them. Naturally, she would say yes. And in no time at all she'd be settled in Sarah's beautiful four-poster bed, watching the flames flicker in the perfect fireplace till she drifted off to sleep.

Three

"WHEN'S SHE COMING?" Lutie asked. The girls were huddled over Cokes at the Burger Master across from school. Sarah didn't want to go home.

"Tomorrow morning. My mother and dad are going over there in our car, and my mother's going to ride back with Aunt Margaret in the nursing-home van. Some of her stuff is at our house already."

"In your bedroom!" Lutie's brown eyes were wide with sympathy. "I just can't believe your folks would do a thing like that . . . make you move from that beautiful bedroom to that crowded little storeroom. You're just like Cinderella, Sarah. They could make a movie about you."

Sarah stared out the window at the snow. She felt like Cinderella.

"There isn't any other way to do it," she said, struggling to be fair. "The storeroom is the only

19

place left." The words released a new flood of bitterness. "Besides, my room is the one Aunt Margaret wants, and what she wants she gets. The minute my mother invited her to come to stay with us, she started talking about my room and how happy she'd be to sleep in it again. She never even asked who was using it now."

Lutie took a last noisy pull on her straw. "I think she sounds awful," she said. "A mean old witch!"

Sarah shrugged. She'd met Aunt Margaret four times in the year her great-aunt had been living at Menlo Manor, and she hadn't seemed particularly witchlike during those visits. She'd just asked all the questions old people always asked: "How old are you?" "What grade are you in?" "Do you like school?" After that they'd had little to say to each other. Sarah and Lloyd had just sat and waited while their parents talked. Mr. and Mrs. Prescott visited Aunt Margaret regularly, and Sarah wondered what they could find to talk about, week after week.

"I don't know what she's like," she said finally. "I'm tired of thinking about her, and she hasn't even moved in yet."

It was a fact that the Prescotts had thought and talked about little else since Monday afternoon when Sarah's mother had visited the nursing home and invited Aunt Margaret to live with them. That night they had begun carrying Sarah's belongings down the hall to the storeroom at the rear of the house.

"As soon as Aunt Margaret is settled, we'll start fixing up this room for you," Mrs. Prescott had promised. "All the boxes and trunks can go up to the attic, and I'll make some fresh curtains for the window. The walls could use a coat of paint, too."

Sarah tossed an armful of clothes on the narrow bed and started back for more. "It doesn't matter," she'd replied dully and heard her mother's sigh behind her.

Remembering that sigh now made Sarah uncomfortable. "Want to go home with me for a while?" she suggested. "My mom and my brother will be at the college delivering some typing, and Dad's out job hunting. We can play the radio as loud as we want."

Later, when Sarah tried to recall the precise moment the trouble started, she decided it was that afternoon when she unlocked the front door. The big front hall, usually so welcoming, seemed chilly. Gabe trotted down the hall from the kitchen, head hanging. He whined when Sarah gave him a hug.

"Let's go upstairs," Lutie said. "Maybe I can help you fix up your new room."

Reluctantly, Sarah agreed. At the top of the stairs, both girls stopped and looked into the big front bedroom that had been Sarah's and now belonged to Aunt Margaret. Sarah saw that her mother had been cleaning. The white curtains were crisp and fresh, and the hardwood floor shone around the blue carpet. Logs and kindling were neatly piled in the fireplace grate, ready for a welcoming fire.

"What's all that stuff on your dresser?" Lutie asked.

The girls crossed the room for a closer look. They stood silently, looking at the vase full of silk sweet peas, the little china boxes, and a framed photograph of two old people. The unfamiliar objects on her dresser made Sarah feel like an intruder.

"That's Aunt Margaret's mother and father," Sarah said. "My dad's grandparents. She had that picture on the table next to her bed at the nursing home. And this, too." She picked up a delicate porcelain figurine, a shepherd leaning on his staff.

"Well, the dresser looked a lot prettier with your things on it," Lutie said. "Who cares about an old shepherd?" She turned away impatiently. "Look at Gabe. He knows this isn't your room anymore. He doesn't even want to come in."

Gabe whined again and followed the girls down the hall to the storeroom. It was still "the storeroom" to Sarah, though she saw that her mother had arranged some bright-colored pillows on the bed. Boxes were stacked on either side of the chest of drawers, and an ancient sewing machine still stood in the corner.

Lutie surveyed the room in silence for a minute. "Well, at least you can put up the painting you liked," she said, pointing to the forest scene that leaned against one wall. "Where are you going to hang it?"

Sarah shrugged. "I don't care," she said. "I don't think I like it as much as I did before."

"That's because you can't hang it over your own fireplace," Lutie said sympathetically. "But it's still a pretty picture, Sarah. Maybe you'll decide to put it up later on."

Sarah doubted it. "It's darker than I thought it was," she said. "Doesn't it look darker to you?"

Lutie narrowed her big brown eyes. "Maybe it's the light," she suggested. "This room isn't as sunny as the other one." She put an arm around Sarah's shoulders and gave her a hug. "Want me to help you carry some of these boxes up to the attic?"

"No, thanks," Sarah said. She didn't want her folks to think the storeroom could ever become an acceptable substitute for the room she had lost. "I don't care what it looks like," she said. "I'm not going to do anything in here but sleep." She grabbed Lutie's wrist and started back down the hall. "My radio's in the kitchen. Let's get some Cokes."

Sarah shivered as she said it, aware, suddenly, that the thought of an ice-cold Coke was not appealing. "Are you cold?" she asked Lutie.

Lutie shook her head. "Just thirsty—and hungry for your Mom's cookies." She was trailing after Sarah but stopped once again at the door of Sarah's old bedroom.

"Oh, no! Look!"

Sarah was already starting down the stairs, but Lutie's exclamation brought her back quickly. The girls stood in the doorway, staring into the room in dismay.

The porcelain shepherd lay on the carpet, face down. His staff was a few inches away, broken into three pieces.

"How could that happen?" Lutie whispered. "Maybe the dog—"

Sarah shook her head. "He didn't go in the room, remember?"

"Well, then," Lutie searched for an explanation, "when you picked it up, you must have put it down too close to the edge of the dresser, Sarah."

"I put it right where I found it," Sarah said sharply. "It was in the middle and in back, next to the picture." She crossed the room quickly and picked up the pieces of the figurine. "My dad can glue these together," she said. "He can fix anything."

"But I still don't see how—"

Sarah laid the pieces on the dresser top. She was badly shaken, but she didn't want to show it, not even to her best friend. "It'll be all right," she said, with more confidence than she felt.

"Come on, let's get out of here."

She could feel Lutie watching her curiously as they descended the stairs. It was easy to guess what her friend was thinking.

You're angry with your Aunt Margaret for taking your room, and you wanted to get even. You must have put the shepherd where it was sure to fall. Sarah supposed that was what her mother would think, too.

The kitchen was as chilly as the rest of the house. Sarah switched on a light and went to the refrigerator for Cokes. She put the cans on the table and brought the cookie jar from the counter, without looking at Lutie.

The truth was, Sarah herself wasn't sure what she'd done. She *thought* she'd put the shepherd back in a safe place, but maybe she hadn't. Maybe—just maybe—it had fallen, and shattered, for the ugly reason Lutie suspected.

Four

H<small>EY, THAT'S COOL!</small>" Lloyd and Sarah were at a living room window, watching the van deliver its passenger. A door opened, a platform slid out, and the wheelchair descended slowly to the ground.

"You can't even see Aunt Margaret!" Lloyd chuckled. "She's all wrapped up like a mummy."

The driver moved the wheelchair away from the curb and then turned to help Mrs. Prescott out of the van. Sarah backed away from the window as the little procession started up the walk. Lloyd raced to open the door. He'd been excited all morning, darting from window to window to see if the van was coming.

He gets in a state over anything! Sarah thought scornfully. She listened to the bustle in the entrance hall—people talking, Gabe barking. The driver said good-bye and strode down the walk, his breath making white puffs in the icy air. Still she lingered in the living room, unwilling to join the others.

"Sarah, where are you? Aunt Margaret is here."

As if I didn't know! With dragging steps Sarah went out to the hall, where her mother was unwrapping the outer layers of shawls that protected the new arrival.

"Hi, Aunt Margaret." Sarah stood awkwardly in front of the wheelchair.

The cotton-white head remained bent, as the old lady struggled to unbutton her coat. Lloyd watched with interest and Sarah with dismay as the gnarled and twisted fingers finally gave up, and Sarah's mother finished the unbuttoning.

She's like a little kid, Sarah thought. *She can't help herself at all.*

The bright blue eyes were anything but childlike, however, when Aunt Margaret finally looked up. "Why aren't you children in school?" she demanded. "Is this Saturday?"

"It's Wednesday," Lloyd said. "The teachers are having meetings all day. They get together and talk about stuff."

"I know what meetings are, young man." Aunt Margaret saw Lloyd staring at her hands, and she thrust them into the sleeves of her sweater. "I was a teacher for thirty-seven years myself. No, don't take the sweater, Ruth." She shrugged

Mrs. Prescott's hands away. "It's cold in here. I suppose the children leave the doors standing open."

"How about a tour of the house, Aunt Margaret?" Mrs. Prescott suggested, with a warning glance at Sarah. "Mrs. Ackerman says you remember every nook and cranny."

"Tina Ackerman talks too much," Aunt Margaret replied. But she didn't protest when Mrs. Prescott pushed the wheelchair into the living room and then down the hall to the big bright kitchen.

"This was our gathering place when I was a girl." The old voice was gentler now. "The cupboards were brown then, not yellow. And we had a nice big wood stove that warmed the whole kitchen." She twisted in her chair to look at Mrs. Prescott. "We had a cook-housekeeper, and there was a cleaning lady who came in three times a week. How much help do you have, Ruth?"

"I have my family. They're very good about doing chores."

Aunt Margaret sniffed. "Well, I should hope so. Otherwise, you're never going to be able to keep up this place and take care of me, too."

Sarah rolled her eyes. It sounded as if Aunt Margaret *planned* to make plenty of work for everyone.

"Well, it'll probably work out." Now the old lady seemed to be reassuring herself. "Sarah is a big girl—she ought to be able to do a lot of the housework. And some of the cooking. Though children are different these days." She looked around the kitchen once more and then, abruptly, she folded in upon herself like a rag doll.

"I am so tired," she said. "I think I'd better get to bed."

"Oh, dear!" Mrs. Prescott clasped her hands in a nervous gesture. "Dave will be home in a few minutes, Aunt Margaret. He'll get you upstairs to your room. I'm afraid the children and I can't do it alone."

"You should have had that driver-person take me up," Aunt Margaret said. "Plenty of time to look around the house some other day. My back feels as if it's breaking." Sarah saw that the lined face had become chalk-white, and the blue eyes had lost their sparkle.

"Maybe she could rest in the living room till Dad comes," Sarah suggested. Surely she and her mother could lift that tiny body from the chair to the couch.

"That's a good idea!" Mrs. Prescott sounded relieved.

"I'll push the chair," Lloyd offered, but Aunt Margaret waved him away. "You're too little— you'll bump into things," she said. When he looked hurt, she reached out and touched his wrist. "I can't stand bumps," she explained, sounding almost, but not quite, apologetic.

It was Sarah who guided the wheelchair into the living room while her mother went upstairs for pillows and a blanket. Then the two of them began the delicate job of maneuvering Aunt Margaret from the chair to the couch. By the time she was lying back against the pillows, they were breathless.

"Now just let me rest for a while," Aunt Margaret ordered. "All this moving around is more than I can take."

"It's time we started lunch, anyway," Mrs. Prescott said. "Come on, Sarah, you can make us some of your famous pancakes."

If she'd hoped to impress Aunt Margaret with Sarah's housekeeping abilities, it didn't work. "None for me," the old lady called after them. "Pancakes give me gas."

Lloyd went outside to repair the snow-robot he'd built after the last storm, and Sarah and her mother retreated to the kitchen. Sarah kept sneaking glances at her mother as they worked. There was something disturbing about that stiff, unwavering smile.

"Go ahead with the pancakes," Mrs. Prescott whispered. "Aunt Margaret can have some home-made soup. She'll enjoy that."

Unless it gives her gas, Sarah said to herself. She had a question to ask her mother, but the possibility that they might be overheard was too great. Finally she wrote it on the little blackboard next to the back door.

Have you told Aunt M. about the shepherd?

Mrs. Prescott shook her head. She picked up the chalk and wrote, *In basement—glue drying. Tell her later. Don't worry.* Then she erased the board thoroughly and went back to fixing a tray.

Sarah broke an egg into the pancake batter. It was easy to say "Don't worry," but she dreaded her great-aunt's reaction to the news. Sarah's parents hadn't argued when she'd insisted the accident was not her fault, but they hadn't looked convinced, either. When Aunt Margaret found out her precious shepherd was broken and Sarah had been the last person to handle it, she'd have plenty to say.

"Ruth!" The shrill cry made Sarah jump. "Come here! Something's the matter with your dog!"

Sarah lifted the frying pan off the burner and darted down the hall with Mrs. Prescott right behind her. They both stopped short in the front hall and stared in astonishment.

Gabe stood at the foot of the stairs looking upward, legs braced, teeth bared. The sound rumbling deep in his chest was terrifying. Sarah had never heard him snarl before.

"What in the world is going on out there?" Aunt Margaret cried from the living room.

Sarah darted forward and looked up the staircase.

"What is it, Sarah?" Mrs. Prescott seemed

unable to move. "Is someone there?"

Sarah shook her head. "I can't see anybody."

"But the dog!" Mrs. Prescott gasped. "Look at him! Listen to him!"

Gabe was rigid with—was it anger or fear? The tail that hardly ever stopped wagging was not wagging now.

"Maybe we should go up and look around." Sarah took a step backward as she said it.

"I asked you what's going on?" Aunt Margaret sounded cross. "Someone come in here and tell me at once."

Mrs. Prescott took Sarah's hand and pulled her toward the living room. "We're all going to stay downstairs together," she whispered. "Till your father comes home. Gabe can stand there and snarl as long as he wants to."

Five

"Ruth, IF YOU THINK there's a burglar upstairs, you should call the police." Aunt Margaret had the blanket pulled up to her chin and appeared ready to dive under it completely at any moment.

"I *don't* think there's anyone up there." Mrs. Prescott said. "But Gabe is behaving so oddly—" Her frown vanished as the back door opened and Sarah's father called hello. Gabe raced to the kitchen, with Sarah and her mother right behind him.

"Dad!" Sarah dragged him down the hall. "Gabe saw someone upstairs. What'll we do?"

"We don't know he saw any such thing," Mrs. Prescott protested. "He just started growling and we don't know why. Maybe you should—"

"Right." Mr. Prescott put a finger to his lips and listened intently for a moment. Then he went up the stairs, two at a time, his red scarf flying.

The overhead floors creaked as he went swiftly from room to room. Closet doors opened and closed, and his footsteps thudded up and down the attic stairs. He was smiling when he finally reappeared at the top of the stairs.

"All clear! Rack up one false alarm for our mighty watchdog."

"Thank goodness!" Mrs. Prescott clutched her forehead. "I could shoot that beast!"

"You tell Davey to come in here," Aunt Margaret cried. "He hasn't even said hello to me."

Davey? Sarah had never heard her father called that before. Mr. Prescott winked at Sarah when he came downstairs. He didn't seem to mind being treated like a little boy.

Sarah and her mother returned to the kitchen, where Gabe was dozing peacefully under the table.

Mrs. Prescott shook her head. "He gets everyone else upset over nothing," she said, "and then he goes to sleep."

Sarah didn't comment. She kept remembering how Gabe had looked standing there at the foot of the stairs, and how ferocious he'd sounded. He had seen something—she was sure of it. In those few minutes, the house itself had changed for Sarah. Since the day they moved in, it had been her family's safe retreat. This was the first time she'd realized that danger might find a way in.

"She's sleeping," Sarah told Lutie a few hours

later. They'd met at their favorite spot in front of the fountain in the mall. "My dad carried her upstairs, and she's all settled."

"In your bed!" Lutie exclaimed. "That's awful!" But her mind was only partly on Sarah's story of the morning's events. "My mother says I can buy white jeans if they're on sale," she reported. "I'm going to save them for the Cavemen concert. Want to help me look?"

"Sure." Sarah tried to sound enthusiastic. Ordinarily, she loved shopping—for herself or anybody else—but today her mind was on what was happening at home. "I have to be back at four to stay with Aunt Margaret while my mother goes over to the college," she said. "That gives us a little more than an hour."

"Plenty of time," Lutie said. "What are you going to wear to the concert?"

Sarah knew that was another way of asking whether she'd talked to her parents about going. "I don't know yet," she said vaguely.

"We'll have to reserve our tickets pretty soon," Lutie continued. "It's just six weeks away and it's probably going to be a sellout."

"I know." Sarah didn't need reminding. In another couple of days, she told herself, she'd ask her parents about the concert. Maybe by then her father would have a new job, but whether he did nor not, she had to make them understand how important this was. A once-in-a-lifetime opportunity—that was how the advertisements described it.

The girls started walking, studying every window, turning in at the stores that specialized in clothes for teens. Christmas decorations, which had started going up before Halloween, had turned the mall into a glittering avenue. Sarah took a deep breath and relaxed. She enjoyed the smells that drifted from the shops—leather and perfume, popcorn and hot pretzels—and it was fun meeting friends from school. If she stayed long enough, walked far enough, Sarah guessed she'd meet everyone she knew.

When she looked at her watch again, it was twenty minutes to four. "I have to go!" she exclaimed, startled at how quickly the time had passed.

"Not yet," Lutie wailed. "I want to look in one more store."

But Sarah didn't dare wait. Her mother had an appointment at the college, and she wouldn't leave the house till Sarah got there.

"You go ahead," she told Lutie. "I'll call you tomorrow." She darted away without waiting for an answer and dashed to the bus stop.

Mrs. Prescott was at the front door when Sarah burst in. "You cut it close," she said mildly. "I'm taking Lloyd with me—we should be back in an hour. I want time to make something good for your father for dinner. Job hunting is a discouraging business."

"I don't want to go with you," Lloyd shouted from the kitchen. "I'm busy."

"You're going," his mother replied. "Sarah can't be responsible for Aunt Margaret and for you, too. Get your coat on, young man."

He might as well get used to it, Sarah thought grimly. Aunt Margaret's arrival was going to change all their lives.

"I checked on her an hour ago," Mrs. Prescott said, as if she'd read Sarah's thoughts. "But you'd better run up now and see if she'd like a cup of tea or something."

Sarah stood at the window and watched her mother and brother trudge down the snowy street. Then she took off her coat and scarf and hung them in the closet. The hall seemed cold, and the chill deepened as she climbed the stairs. *Weird,* she thought. The house had always warmed slowly in the morning, but once warm it stayed snugly comfortable all day.

"Is that you, Ruth?"

"It's Sarah, Aunt Margaret." She hesitated at the door of the bedroom—*her* bedroom—and took in the changes. Aunt Margaret's television set was on the old trunk where Sarah's oversized teddy bear used to sit. A water pitcher and a glass with

a straw in it stood on the bedside table, and there
was a row of medicine bottles and pill containers
behind them. The wheelchair was near the bed, a
pale pink shawl thrown over the back.

The room even smelled different, Sarah
thought—kind of stuffy.

"I need another blanket." Aunt Margaret looked
smaller than ever in the middle of the big four-
poster. "I'm freezing to death," she added accus-
ingly.

Sarah hurried down the hall to the linen closet
and came back with a thick woolen blanket that
her uncle and aunt had sent from Canada.

"Not that," Aunt Margaret said sharply. "It's
too heavy for my poor bones. Isn't there something
lighter—a comforter, maybe?"

Sarah hesitated. The only comforter in the house
was the pale blue one on her own bed. It had
been her parents' birthday present to her last
year.

"Oh, well, if you don't have one, you don't
have one," Aunt Margaret said. "Cold makes me
ache, but heavy covers do, too. I'll just have to
put up with it, I suppose."

"We have a comforter," Sarah admitted. "I'll
get it." She knew her conscience would prick her
if she didn't.

When Sarah returned, Aunt Margaret eyed the
comforter with approval. "That's lovely," she

said. "Thank you very much." She smiled—a crooked little smile revealing shiny false teeth.

Sarah spread the comforter over the bed. "Would you like a cup of tea?" she asked. "Mom said I should ask you."

Aunt Margaret peered over the expanse of pale blue. Her thin fingers toyed with the stitching around the edge of the comforter. "What I'd like," she said slowly, "is to find out what's happened to my Dresden shepherd. I *told* your mother to pack it, but it's not here. She must have left it behind."

Sarah gulped. She'd hoped that by now her mother had explained that the shepherd had met with an accident.

"It's my dearest possession," Aunt Margaret went on. "I got it from my mother when I was a child, and it always stood there on my dresser. When I moved to California, I took it with me. It was like having a little bit of home."

"It's here." Sarah blurted out her story, afraid that if she slowed down she might not have the nerve to finish. "It fell on the floor and broke, but Dad fixed it. It's downstairs in his workroom now."

Aunt Margaret gave a little cry of dismay. "What do you mean, it fell?" she demanded. "Did Ruth drop it?"

"Nobody dropped it," Sarah said. "It just—

fell." The explanation sounded as weak now as it had when she'd told her parents what happened.

"Then it couldn't have been put in a safe place," Aunt Margaret snapped. "Things don't fall by themselves."

"But it did," Sarah protested. "I put it right in the middle of the dresser—"

"*You* put it," Aunt Margaret interrupted. "You mean you were handling it."

"I just wanted to look at it." Sarah could imagine Aunt Margaret cross-examining naughty children in her classroom in just this way.

"Well, then . . ." The gnarled hands suddenly retreated under the comforter. "What time is it?" she demanded.

Sarah looked at her watch. "It's nearly four-thirty."

"Then I can have a pain pill now." Aunt Sarah said. "I can have one every four hours, and I had the last one right after lunch."

Sarah examined the pill containers till she found one marked "Every four hours as needed for pain." She showed it to Aunt Margaret. "Is this the one?"

Aunt Margaret nodded.

"Are you hurting?"

The old lady sniffed. "I'm always hurting. Arthritis is a terrible thing. No, put the pill in that little cup, and give it to me. Don't expect me to hold it in my fingers."

Sarah handed her the cup and then helped her to steady the glass of water at her lips.

When the pill had gone down, Aunt Margaret lay back. "Davey will have to keep the house warmer than this," she said. "I'm still cold. Don't you feel it?"

Sarah nodded. "Sort of." She was wondering if Aunt Margaret was really in pain all the time. That must be terrible.

"Either you're cold or you aren't. There's no 'sort of.'" Aunt Margaret closed her eyes. "I'm going to take a nap now."

"Okay." Sarah was glad to be dismissed. She refilled the water glass and was almost out the door when the old lady spoke again.

"You just remember what I said. Honesty is the best policy."

Sarah whirled around. Aunt Margaret's eyes were still closed.

"I don't know what you mean."

"I mean it's better to admit you dropped my Dresden shepherd than to pretend you didn't. Lying is a very bad habit."

Sarah was outraged, her sympathy for Aunt Margaret's pain forgotten. "That's not fair!" she exclaimed. "I don't lie!"

"And things don't fall on the floor by themselves," Aunt Margaret retorted. "Now let me sleep."

Sarah stood in the doorway, fuming, for a

moment or two, and then she stormed downstairs. *Mean old thing!* she thought. One thing was sure. Having Aunt Margaret live with them wasn't just going to be hard: It was going to be absolutely awful.

Six

I JUST CAN'T IMAGINE you clerking in a convenience store," Mrs. Prescott said. She was spooning tomato sauce over a platter of spaghetti. "You've always despised grocery shopping."

"Well, I can't say I've suddenly learned to love it," Sarah's father said dryly. "I just don't have much choice. It's a job. It'll bring in some money, and by working the second shift I'll have most of the day free to keep looking." He turned to Sarah and Lloyd. "What do you kids think of the idea?"

Sarah shrugged. "It's okay, I guess."

When her father announced that he had a job, her first thought had been that now it would be all right to mention the Cavemen concert again. Then he'd told them what his wages would be, and she realized this was not the time to ask a favor.

43

"I think it's neat," Lloyd announced. "Will you get free bubble gum?"

Mr. Prescott chuckled and twirled spaghetti around his fork. "It won't be free, but I think I might bring home a twenty-four hour supply tonight—*if* you go with your mother to the college without making a fuss."

Lloyd groaned. "Again?"

Mrs. Prescott shook her head at him. "I'm sorry, but that's the way it has to be. I have to check out a few things before I finish typing this report, and I'm not going to leave you at home with Sarah. She's doing her share by looking after Aunt Margaret while your father and I are away."

"I don't need a baby-sitter," Lloyd grumbled.

Sarah felt sorry for him. Aunt Margaret had been with them for four nights, and on three of those Lloyd had had to go to the college or to the library with their mother. She didn't blame him for complaining, but she felt sorry for herself, too.

"How long will you be gone?" she asked.

"An hour or so," her mother said. "You have homework, don't you?"

Sarah nodded.

"Aunt Margaret took an extra pain pill at five because her knees and fingers hurt so much," Mrs. Prescott said. "She'll probably sleep while we're gone. And even if she wakes up, she seems to enjoy being alone. I think she missed her privacy at the nursing home."

Sarah and Aunt Margaret had scarcely spoken to each other since that first night. Except for an occasional request for a glass of warm milk or an extra pillow, the old lady had made it clear that she could manage by herself—and that suited Sarah perfectly.

It wasn't the "baby-sitting" but something quite different that was making Sarah dread her evenings alone.

The first time she'd heard the sound was two nights ago. She'd been sitting at the kitchen table, trying to concentrate on the Battle of Gettysburg, when it began—a slow *tap-tap, tap-tap,* that seemed to come from the closet in the back hall. Gabe was asleep at her feet; she poked him with a toe, but he just yawned and moved farther away.

The tapping continued—getting louder, then fading, then getting louder again. Sarah forced herself to cross the kitchen to the hall and open the closet door. The minute she touched the knob, the tapping stopped. Mops, brooms, vacuum cleaner, shelves of polishes and cleaners—there was nothing inside to explain that odd knocking.

Last night it had happened again, but this time the sound came from the coat closet in the front hall. Once again, it stopped as soon as she touched the knob. She'd stared at the row of coats and jackets, her heart thudding.

She didn't mention the tapping the first night.

She had, in fact, forgotten about it by the time her mother and Lloyd came home, tramping snow from their boots and eager for hot cocoa and gingerbread. But last night she was still shaken when her mother returned. As soon as they came in the door, she began describing what had happened, stopping only when Mrs. Prescott made a weary gesture.

"I can't imagine what you heard, but I'm sure it was nothing to worry about," she'd said. "Don't make a big deal of it, Sarah."

Lloyd was more interested. "I told you so," he crowed. "This really is a haunted house."

"Don't be silly!" Mrs. Prescott set her boots to dry in the hall and returned to the kitchen. "I hope you didn't say anything about this to Aunt Margaret," she said. "She seems contented here now, but she won't be for long if you get her all worked up about nothing at all."

Sarah wondered how her mother knew Aunt Margaret was contented. "I haven't told her anything," she said sulkily. "She doesn't like me."

"That's nonsense," Mrs. Prescott scolded. "Why wouldn't she like you?"

"She thinks I broke her precious shepherd and lied about it."

Sarah's mother looked pained. "I'm sure that's not true. The figurine is back on her dresser, and she agrees that your father did a beautiful repair job. She's forgotten all about it."

"Anyway," Sarah persisted, "what do you think the tapping noise was, Mom?"

"Wind," Mrs. Prescott answered promptly. "A mouse in the wall. Who knows? Nothing to worry about."

Remembering that conversation, Sarah knew what her mother had left unsaid. *We have bigger things to be concerned about than an unexplained noise in the walls of an old house. Your dad has to find a good job, and I have to take care of a sick old lady. Let's not fret about little things!*

Now Mrs. Prescott and Lloyd were on their way to the college again, and Sarah was going to be alone. A few minutes later, Mr. Prescott came into the living room to say good-bye.

"I'm going to spend a few hours at the store each evening to find out how things are done," he explained. "Next week I'll start a regular shift." He hesitated, looking around the comfortable room as though he hated to leave it. "I'm going to miss my evenings at home."

Sarah jumped up from the sofa and gave her father a hug. "I'll miss you, too," she said. "I *hate* being alone."

"But you're not really alone," her father said. "Aunt Margaret's here."

As if that made it easier.

After he left, Sarah curled up on the sofa again, her textbooks beside her. The house was very quiet; Mrs. Prescott had specifically warned her

not to turn on the radio. Aunt Margaret had a little
bell at her bedside, in case she woke up and
needed help. The radio might drown out the bell.

The weekend math assignment was hard. Sarah
struggled with it for a while, then put her notebook
aside. She'd do her homework for English class
first. Later, after her mother and Lloyd came home,
she'd call Lutie and they could figure out the math
together.

The English assignment was to write an essay
on December. Sarah started slowly, gathering her
thoughts about what the month meant to her. This
would be her family's first Christmas in a big
house, and she'd been looking forward to making
it beautiful for the holiday. *We live in a house that
was just made for Christmas decorations. . . .* She
stopped writing to wonder if there would be money
for the ropes of pine boughs she'd hoped to wind
around the bannister and loop over the fireplaces.
And could they afford a really big tree? Probably
not.

She cuddled into the corner of the high-backed
sofa. The house was really chilly tonight. She
wondered if her parents had started turning down
the thermostat to save fuel.

*I like snow, but I don't like shoveling. I like
icicles when I can look at them from inside a
warm place. . . .* She shivered again. The room
was getting colder every minute.

A sound in the kitchen made her hold her breath, until she recognized the clicking of Gabe's toenails on the hall floor. The big dog came into the living room and stood in front of Sarah for a moment. Then he circled the room, moving slowly, head cocked as if he were listening for something.

"Stop that," Sarah said. Her voice sounded loud in the quiet house. She tried to go back to her essay. *Once my brother and I made a snowman and dressed him in some old clothes we found in a trunk. He looked so real that our dog attacked him. . . .*

Gabe was in the front hall now and standing at the foot of the stairs. As Sarah watched, his body stiffened and he began to growl. She dropped her notebook and stood up.

"Gabe, come here!"

He didn't move. She started toward him, then froze as the floor creaked overhead. The sound came again and then again—not the ordinary shiftings and stirrings of an old house on a cold night, but a steady series of creaks.

Footsteps.

Gabe began to snarl, the same deep-throated warning sounds Sarah had heard the day Aunt Margaret moved in. Someone was moving around upstairs. Any second now, Aunt Margaret would wake up and hear it, too.

Sarah walked on tiptoe across the living room,

past Gabe and down the hall to the kitchen.
With trembling fingers she dialed the emergency
number 911.

"There's someone in our house," she whispered into the phone. "I don't know what to do."

The woman's voice on the other end of the line
was reassuringly calm. She asked Sarah's name
and address and whether she was home alone.
Sarah answered through clenched teeth, while the
footsteps continued overhead.

"We'll have a squad car there in five minutes,
maybe sooner," the woman promised. "You go
outside and wait. Go to a neighbor's house."

"I can't," Sarah whispered hoarsely. "My great-
aunt—she's sick in bed—"

"If there's an intruder in your house, the best
thing you can do is leave. Please do as I tell you.
The police are already on their way."

"Okay." She hung up the phone and tiptoed
back down the hall. Gabe was still at the foot of
the stairs, but his snarl had faded to a grumble.
The footsteps had stopped. Sarah wondered if
someone was at the top of the stairs just out of
sight, listening as she was listening, waiting to
see if she would come up to investigate.

I can't, she thought. *I just can't.* She started to
back away, snatching her jacket from the closet
as she passed. Still facing the stairs, she opened
the front door and stepped out onto the porch.

That was as far as she would go. She couldn't

leave Aunt Margaret alone, no matter what the
emergency operator said. If she wakened and
rang her bell . . . *Oh, please don't let her ring the
bell!*

The night was crisp and white under a full
moon. Sarah held the door open so she could hear
if Aunt Margaret wanted her. This strange behavior
obviously puzzled Gabe, and after a couple of
glances over his shoulder, he dashed past her and
out into the yard. When the police car pulled up
a minute later, its red and blue lights flashing, he
was at the curb to welcome the two men who
jumped out.

Sarah stepped aside to let the policemen into
the hall. "Up there," she pointed. "Somebody
was walking around, but now he's stopped. My
great-aunt's asleep in the front bedroom."

One of the officers started up the steps; the
other—curly-haired and freckled—paused.
"You're Sarah Prescott?"

Sarah nodded.

"Well, you stay down here, Sarah. If your aunt
wakes up and is frightened, we'll call you. And
keep your dog outside. Okay?"

She nodded again.

"Good girl." He climbed the stairs swiftly, and
she saw him look in at Aunt Margaret's door.

Sarah listened to the two men moving from
room to room, opening and closing closets, just
as her father had searched a few nights ago. He

hadn't found anyone, but this time—

The door opened behind her, so unexpectedly that Sarah's trembling knees almost gave way. Her mother and Lloyd burst in, with Gabe right behind them.

"Sarah! What in the world is going on here? There's a police car in front of the house!" Mrs. Prescott gasped as the two officers appeared at the top of the stairs. "Oh, no! Is it Margaret?"

"No, Mom," Sarah said hurriedly. "I got scared because I heard someone moving around upstairs. I called the emergency number."

"Wow!" Lloyd was impressed.

The policemen came downstairs, trying to move quietly but not succeeding very well. "Your aunt is okay, ma'am," the freckled officer said. "Still sleeping, in fact. And there's no sign of a break-in. It was a false alarm." He glanced at Sarah's white face and added hastily, "But your daughter did the right thing. Better not to take chances."

Mrs. Prescott looked bewildered. "You mean you actually thought you heard someone walking up there, Sarah?"

"And Gabe was snarling again," Sarah said. "Just the way he did the other night."

The policemen exchanged glances. "Are you saying this has happened before?" the other officer asked. "We don't have a record of another call."

"My husband checked the first time," Mrs. Prescott said faintly. "There was nothing—no one.

l'm sorry Sarah bothered you."

"No problem, ma'am." The policeman's tone was still courteous, but he looked as if he was trying not to grin. "l have a kid with a lively imagination, too. l always warn him, don't watch spooky plays on TV or read ghost stories when you're home alone, but does he listen? No way!"

Sarah's face grew hot. "l wasn't doing either one of those things!" she exclaimed. "l was just working on my homework when l heard someone upstairs."

"Only you didn't *really* hear anyone, did you?" Mrs. Prescott sounded exasperated. "Since there's no one there."

"What about Gabe?" Sarah demanded. "He heard someone, too."

"Who knows what is going on in this dog's head?" her mother snapped. "We certainly can't call the police every time Gabe feels the need for a little excitement in his life."

"Hey, maybe it was a ghost," Lloyd suggested. "l bet it was! l hope it was!"

Mrs. Prescott groaned, and the two policemen laughed. They were still chuckling as they said good-bye.

"l'm going to check on Aunt Margaret," Mrs. Prescott said, breaking the painful silence the policemen left behind them. She tiptoed upstairs, leaving Sarah and Lloyd to stare at each other in the hall.

"Do you think it *was* a ghost, Sarah?" Lloyd's eyes were very big.

Sarah shrugged. She was embarrassed and scared, and she didn't want to talk about it.

"Well, I hope it was a ghost," Lloyd answered himself. "I'm going to tell everybody—"

He broke off with a wary glance upward. Mrs. Prescott was coming back down the steps.

"You're not going to tell anybody anything, young man," she said. "If I catch either one of you frightening Aunt Margaret with that kind of crazy talk. . . . I can hardly believe she slept through those big men tramping around up there, but she did. She would have been absolutely terrified if she'd seen them."

Suddenly Sarah thought she knew what her mother was thinking. "You're saying I called the police because I *wanted* to scare Aunt Margaret!" she exclaimed. "You think I just pretended I heard someone walking up there."

Mrs. Prescott looked troubled. "It doesn't sound like you," she said. "But all this talk of footsteps— and tapping in closets—you never let your imagination run wild before Aunt Margaret came, Sarah. And you never minded staying home alone. Can you blame me for thinking there may be some connection?"

Sarah stared at her mother, too stunned to defend herself.

Mrs. Prescott took off her coat and hung it in

the closet. "What you'd better remember," she said slowly, "is that if you frighten Aunt Margaret into wanting to go back to Menlo Manor, she won't be the only one to leave. Your father's doing the very best he can, but he isn't earning enough now to pay the rent here. If Aunt Margaret goes, we'll be out of this house ourselves, as soon as we can find something cheaper."

Seven

PROMISE ME YOU WON'T TELL anyone else. Promise!"
Sarah walked backwards in the cafeteria lunch
line so she could face Lutie.

"But it's so exciting, Sarah!" Lutie protested.
"I never knew anyone who lived in a haunted
house before. I should think you'd want to tell."

"Well, I don't." The line stopped abruptly, and
Sarah crashed into Jason Briggs.

"Hey, watch it!" Jason grabbed his wedge of
pizza as it started to slide off his tray. "Look
where you're going, will ya!"

"Sorry." She turned to walk sideways and
helped herself to pizza and an apple. "I don't
want anybody but you to know, Lutie," she
repeated. "You're my best friend, so it's okay."
But already she was beginning to be sorry she'd
mentioned the tapping in the closets and the
mysterious footsteps. She felt as if she'd been

disloyal to her house by admitting something peculiar was happening there.

The cafeteria was always noisy, but today the din had risen to a new pitch. Sarah and Lutie carried their trays to a far corner where Megan Draper and Heather Thoms were saving places for them.

"Lucky you." Megan was looking at Sarah's pizza. "I have a cheese sandwich from home, and the cheese is stiff. Yuk!"

"I was supposed to make a sandwich, too, but I didn't have time," Sarah said.

"Why not?" Lutie asked the question so eagerly that Megan and Heather glanced at her in surprise. "Did something else exciting happen?"

Before Sarah could think of an answer, Megan snickered. "The only exciting thing that happens at our house in the morning is my father getting mad because I take too long in the bathroom."

"Or the dog runs away," Heather said. "That happens at our house once a week, at least."

Lutie continued to look at her pleadingly, but Sarah pretended not to notice. She wasn't going to tell about *her* morning, no matter how much Lutie wanted to hear.

The day had begun with Aunt Margaret announcing that her knees and shoulders ached because she'd become chilled during the night. Sarah, sorting through the storeroom closet for a blouse to wear, heard her mother remind Aunt Margaret

that she could have called for another blanket or
a shawl.

"How would I do that?" the old lady demanded
tartly. "I don't like shrieking for help like a
banshee in the middle of the night."

"Your bell," Mrs. Prescott said mildly.

"Someone stole it. See for yourself."

There had followed a long silence, while Sarah
stood very still, straining to hear what was happening. *That's dumb,* she told herself. *Who would
steal the bell, for goodness' sake?* She heard her
mother moving around Aunt Margaret's room,
then the sharp click of her heels as she came down
the hall.

"Sarah, Aunt Margaret's bell isn't on her bedside table," Mrs. Prescott announced. "Any
thoughts on where it could be?"

Sarah was still standing at her closet door.

"Why ask me?"

"Don't be sassy." Her mother sounded tired.
"I'm asking you because you sat with Aunt
Margaret last night, and you might have moved the
bell without thinking. I don't remember whether it
was on the bedside table when I got her ready to
sleep."

"Well, I didn't touch it." Sarah knew she was
being rude, but she couldn't help it. From the
moment Aunt Margaret had said the bell was
missing, she'd been sure she would be accused.

Mrs. Prescott stood in the doorway for another

moment or two. Then she'd turned and gone back to the front bedroom, leaving Sarah angry and upset.

Lutie leaned across the cafeteria table, breaking into Sarah's thoughts. "Want some of my sister's birthday cake? I brought extra pieces."

Sarah smiled and shook her head. She didn't feel like eating cake. She didn't even want the pizza and wished she hadn't bought it. Just thinking about this morning made her stomach churn.

Breakfast had been quiet, broken only by Lloyd's chatter. Sarah looked up once from her cereal to find her mother watching her with a sad expression. Later, when they were alone in the kitchen, she'd put an arm around Sarah's shoulders.

"I wasn't accusing you of anything," she said softly. "If it sounded that way, I'm sorry."

"That's okay," Sarah said. But it wasn't. When the breakfast dishes were rinsed, she went back upstairs.

Aunt Margaret was propped against her pillows, a tray in front of her. Pain had deepened the lines around her mouth and shadowed her eyes.

"I'm sorry you don't feel good," Sarah said politely.

Aunt Margaret nodded. "You can take this tray," she said. "I'm not hungry."

Sarah lifted the tray from the bed and set it next

to the door to take downstairs later. "My mom says you can't find your bell," she said.

"That's right. Somebody stole it."

Sarah crossed the room and knelt to look under the bed.

"Ruth already did that," Aunt Margaret snapped. "It wasn't there then, and it won't be there now."

Sarah stood up and began circling the room. She moved the curtains and slid a hand between the cushions of the armchair.

"Your mother looked in all those places," Aunt Margaret said when Sarah stopped at the desk and peered into the pigeonholes.

The fireplace mantel was crowded with old photos of all shapes and sizes. Some were in tarnished silver frames, and others were propped against the chimney. One by one, Sarah picked them up and set them down again.

"That's a waste of time!" Aunt Margaret complained. "I'd rather you didn't handle all my pictures."

"I'm being careful." Sarah didn't want to give up. The bell had to be close by—dropped in some unlikely place when Aunt Margaret needed a pill in a hurry or another pillow behind her aching shoulders. Sarah didn't want to go to school with her mother's suspicions riding around with her all day, like lead in her pocket.

The last picture on the mantel was a portrait of

an old man with wavy white hair. The photo didn't have a frame; it was in one of those stiff gray folders provided by the photographer, with the cover bent backward to make the picture stand by itself. Sarah lifted the photo and dropped it down in a single motion. Then she lifted it again. The bell was there, pushed back into the crease of the folder.

"Well, well," Aunt Margaret said. "That's a surprise! It certainly didn't get way over there by itself, did it?"

Sarah set the bell carefully on the bedside table, next to the television remote control. She knew Aunt Margaret was thinking the same thing her mother had thought earlier—that Sarah must have moved it. She wanted to be as angry with Aunt Margaret as she'd been with her mother. Instead, she was bewildered, and frightened, too. There was no way that the bell could have been dropped accidentally inside the picture-folder. It had been pushed back out of sight. It had been hidden. Sarah knew she wasn't guilty herself, but she couldn't imagine who else might have done such a thing.

The question had stayed with her all morning. Even now, sitting in the crowded cafeteria with her friends, she could think about nothing else.

"What's the matter with you, Sarah?" Megan demanded. "Aren't you going to eat your pizza?"

Sarah pushed her plate away. "You can have it

if you want it," she said. "I'm not hungry."

Her stomach was turning somersaults. As vividly as if it were happening all over again, she saw herself standing next to Aunt Margaret's bed, looking into those piercing blue eyes.

"I didn't move the bell," she'd said earnestly. "I really didn't."

Aunt Margaret sighed. "No, I guess you didn't," she said, after what seemed a very long time. "It would be simpler if I could believe you had."

Sarah wanted to ask what that meant, but at the same time she longed to get away. "I'll tell Mom we found the bell," she said.

Aunt Margaret nodded. "You do that." Suddenly, the anger was drained out of her voice. If it had been anyone but Aunt Margaret, Sarah would have suspected she was close to tears.

The girls had English class together after lunch.

"If we have to read our essays out loud I'll die!" Heather exclaimed. "I hate December."

"Except for Christmas," Lutie said.

"Right. And except that it means it won't be long till the Cavemen concert—but I didn't think I ought to write about that. Oh, I forgot—if you all bring your money tomorrow, my dad said he'll buy the tickets downtown."

Sarah felt Lutie looking at her again. "I'll have to see," she said reluctantly. "I'm not sure I'll be going."

"Not going!" Megan was shocked. "But we've been planning it for months, Sarah. We're all going."

"I know." Sarah walked faster. "I'll have to let you know tomorrow."

"Well, I don't see—"

Sarah was relieved when the bell rang and they turned in to Room 112. She'd have to talk to her parents tonight; there was no way to postpone asking any longer.

It was another reason why she dreaded going home.

Eight

THE KITCHEN WAS FRAGRANT and inviting after the cold walk from school. Six loaves of bread were cooling on the counter and Mrs. Prescott was stirring a kettle of soup. Sarah took a deep breath and felt some of the day's tension fade away.

"It smells great in here."

Her mother nodded, smiling. "There's something about this house," she mused. "It makes me want to do the things other women did here. Like baking bread. Aunt Margaret says her mother did all their baking and made most of Margaret's dresses." She grimaced. "I'd draw the line there, even if I had time to sew. I don't think I'd be very good at whipping up a pair of jeans for my daughter."

Sarah was relieved to find her mother in good spirits. There had been a bad moment at breakfast when Sarah had mentioned that the missing bell was found. Mrs. Prescott had started to say something and then had closed her lips firmly, obviously holding back questions about how the bell could have gotten across the bedroom to the mantel.

"We're going to eat early," she said now. "Your dad has spent the afternoon with a job counselor, and this evening he's going back to the store for several hours." She sighed. "I hate to think this is the last night he'll be home with us for dinner. He starts his regular shift tomorrow."

Sarah took plates from the cupboard and began setting the table. "There's something I have to ask you," she said, not looking at her mother. "It's very important."

"Ask away." Mrs. Prescott tasted the soup. "Just so it doesn't involve spending money."

Sarah's heart sank. "But it does," she blurted. "There's this rock concert in January—I told you about it a while ago. Everybody's going to be there." She tried to remember her carefully marshaled arguments. "It can be one of my Christmas presents. Please!"

Her mother leaned against the counter. "How much is the ticket?" she asked softly.

"Not much."

"How much?"

Sarah took a deep breath. "Thirty-five dollars."

The silence seemed to last forever. Then Mrs. Prescott turned back to the stove. "I don't think you have any idea how serious our financial situation is, Sarah," she said. "If you did, you wouldn't even bring this up. We're looking for money to buy shoes, and to buy gasoline, and fuel to keep this big house warm. And food, for goodness' sake! How can you even think about a thirty-five-dollar concert ticket?"

"It can be my *only* Christmas present!" Sarah knew she was whining, but she couldn't help it.

"You need new boots. *Need* is the only word that counts this Christmas. I'm sorry."

Sarah swallowed hard. "I *need* this," she said. "You're going to ruin my life if you say no. I'll be the only one who won't be there."

Her mother came around the table and gave her a hug. "I really am sorry," she said. "But that's the way it is." She turned Sarah so they were face to face. "And you're not to say one word about this to your father. He feels bad enough about losing his job, without your making him feel guilty."

Sarah wrenched free and ran out of the kitchen. "It's not fair," she shouted over her shoulder. "I had to give up my room, and now I have to give up the concert, too. Nobody cares what I want!"

"Sarah!"

"It's true!" She raced upstairs past Aunt Margaret's open door and down the hall. Her storeroom-bedroom was so crowded that she had to move a box before she could slam the door.

She threw herself on the narrow bed and sobbed. Her mother didn't understand the importance of the concert. It wasn't just that she'd miss the only personal appearance the Cavemen might ever make in Milwaukee. It was going to the concert with Lutie and Megan and Heather that mattered.

During her first week at Pioneer Middle School Sarah had sat alone in the cafeteria each noon. In the second week, just when she'd thought she'd die of loneliness, Lutie had stopped and asked if she'd like to eat lunch with her and her friends. Sarah felt as if a light had been turned on, flooding the yellow-green cafeteria walls with sunshine.

During that first lunch the girls had talked constantly about the Cavemen's concert in January. It was just a rumor then, but a thrilling one. The next day they seemed to take it for granted that Sarah would eat with them again. On the third day, they'd asked her if she was going to the concert, too. She was part of the group.

That was why the concert was important. It was a symbol of all the good things that had happened to her since her family moved to Willow Park. She couldn't bear to give it up.

"We're going to eat now, Sarah. Come along."

The summons woke Sarah from an uneasy sleep. She sat up, blinking in the darkness, and the memory of her talk with her mother came rushing back. Maybe she would skip supper. She hesitated, then remembered the homemade soup.

She opened the door. The fire in Aunt Margaret's fireplace sent a soft glow down the hallway. *My fireplace,* Sarah thought resentfully.

"Is that you, Sarah?" The quavering voice stopped her at the top of the stairs. "Please come in here a moment."

Sarah bit her lip. Aunt Margaret had probably heard her shout that she hadn't wanted to give up her bedroom. Now she was going to tell her what a selfish girl she was. Stiffening her shoulders, Sarah stepped through the doorway. Her great-aunt was in the wheelchair, a supper tray balanced across the arms.

"Your mother makes very good soup."

Sarah nodded, waiting for the scolding to begin.

"I've been thinking about my bell," Aunt Margaret continued. "I keep wondering how it got behind that picture on the mantel."

Disappointment over the Cavemen concert had made Sarah forget, for the moment, the mystery of the bell. "I told you I didn't—" she began, but Aunt Margaret cut her off with a wave of her hand.

"I'm not accusing you of anything. I'm just looking for an explanation. Looking rather desperately, I suppose. Do you think Lloyd might have moved the bell while I was sleeping?"

"Lloyd!" Sarah was astonished at the suggestion. "Why would he do a thing like that?"

"As a joke, perhaps." Aunt Margaret sounded as if she hoped it were true. "Boys his age are full of mischief."

Sarah tried to picture her little brother tiptoeing into Aunt Margaret's room and hiding the bell.

"I'll ask him," she said slowly. "But I don't think he did it."

"Then who?"

"I don't know." Sarah was tired of the question and impatient with the anxiety in her great-aunt's eyes. Aunt Margaret only cared about what happened here in this room. She didn't know the Cavemen existed, and if she did know she wouldn't be interested. "I have to go down to supper," Sarah said. "Don't worry about the bell. It just—it just got misplaced, that's all."

"Misplaced," Aunt Margaret repeated. "How could that be?"

But now she didn't seem to expect an answer. When Sarah looked back from the top of the stairs, the old lady was bent over her soup, inhaling the steam. *In her own little world,* Sarah thought.

The dinner hour was quiet, with Sarah and her mother avoiding each other's eyes. Mr. Prescott was too distracted to notice the silence until the meal was nearly over. Then he looked around with a puzzled air.

"You're glum, Sarah," he said. "What's the matter? Math teacher spring a test?"

Sarah's mother sent her a warning glance.

"I'm okay," Sarah said.

"Good." Her father sounded relieved, as if he didn't really want to hear about any problems.

"Sarah's letting Aunt Margaret use her comforter," Mrs. Prescott said unexpectedly. "The one we gave her for her birthday."

"That's my girl." Mr. Prescott nodded approvingly and then pushed back his chair. "I have to get going—see you later, gang."

When he had left, and their mother had gone upstairs to check on Aunt Margaret, Sarah and Lloyd carried the dishes to the sink.

"I'm going to ask you something, and you'd better tell me the truth," Sarah said. "Did you hide that little bell that belongs next to Aunt Margaret's bed?"

Lloyd looked outraged. "Why would I do that? I don't want her stuff."

"You could have done it," Sarah persisted. "You're the one who's always hoping something spooky will happen so you can tell people you live in a haunted house."

"What's spooky about losing a bell? I lose stuff all the time."

Sarah gave up. She knew Lloyd well enough to be certain he was telling the truth. Obviously, there wasn't going to be an easy explanation for how the bell had traveled from the bedside table to the mantel, so she had better stop looking for one.

Lloyd was right; it wasn't important. What *was* important was that tomorrow she'd have to tell Lutie and Megan and Heather that her parents couldn't afford to let her go to the Cavemen's concert. The girls would feel sorry for her. And next time they were going someplace special, they'd be careful not to let her know, because they wouldn't want to hurt her feelings.

She would no longer be part of the crowd.

She was washing dishes, turning over another idea, when her mother came back downstairs.

"Mom, the night of the concert—"

"Please don't start again."

"I'm not," Sarah said. "I was just going to ask if I could invite the girls for a sleepover after the concert. They like to come here."

Her mother shook her head. "They liked sleeping on bedrolls in front of the fireplace in your bedroom," she said. "That's out of the question now. And don't say you can sleep downstairs in front of the living room fireplace, because it just won't do, Sarah. The chatter and the giggling and all the running around would keep Aunt Margaret awake all night. It wouldn't be fair."

"You mean I can't even have a party? Not ever?" Sarah felt tears starting all over again.

"I didn't say that." Mrs. Prescott seemed to be

struggling to be patient. "But a slumber party is different. Nobody in the family gets much sleep during a slumber party—you know that's true. The rest of us can stand it once in a while, but Aunt Margaret is sick, and she has to put up with a lot of pain. She needs all the sleep she can get."

Sarah started for the hall, but her mother called her back. "One tantrum per evening is enough," she said firmly. "I'm sorry you're unhappy, but you still have your chores to do. It's your turn to wash the dishes, and Lloyd will wipe. I have extra laundry, and then a couple of hours of typing."

When Sarah finally escaped to her room, she felt angry with the whole world.

She switched on the lamp next to the bed and looked around at the clutter. A few feet away, the forest painting stood where she and Lutie had propped it—what a long time ago that seemed! It was hard to believe that only two weeks had passed. Then she'd had nothing more serious on her mind than deciding whether to leave Aunt Margaret's portrait on the wall over the fireplace or replace it with this painting. She wondered why it had mattered so much. She didn't even like the forest picture very much now. It had seemed bright and cheerful to her then, a reminder of happy times, but now it looked somber and dark.

She leaned forward to examine the painting more closely. It was ridiculous to think it had changed, and yet—yes, it really did seem different.

The little forest clearing was full of shadows, as though the artist had painted it just before a storm.

That's silly! she told herself. *The painting hasn't changed. I've changed, myself. My life is full of shadows.*

She could almost hear her mother's snort of disgust. *Self-pity is a waste of time, Sarah. Where would I be if I used up my energy feeling sorry for myself?*

As if to underline that thought, the bell tinkled at the other end of the hall. Sarah clenched her fists and lay still. She knew she ought to get up and find out what Aunt Margaret wanted, but she didn't move. The ringing stopped, then started again, and at last footsteps started up the stairs. Mrs. Prescott climbed slowly, as if she were tired, but her voice was cheerful as she asked Aunt Margaret how she'd like a nice hot cup of cocoa.

Nine

THE TYPEWRITER WAS CHATTERING in the dining room when Sarah got home from school the next afternoon.

"Come in here," her mother called. "I want to show you something."

Sarah hung her jacket in the back hall and went into the dining room. Here mother looked up from her work, smiling.

"Look at that," she gestured at the papers scattered across the table. The late winter sun, shining through the stained-glass panels above the buffet, laid bars of shimmering color across the manuscript.

"Imagine us in a house with a stained-glass window," Mrs. Prescott said. "It's the nine hundred-and-ninety-ninth good thing about living here."

"It's pretty," Sarah agreed. She slid into a chair

and waited, sure that her mother had more on her mind than the beauty of the stained-glass window.

"How was your day?"

"Not bad," Sarah said. "We had tests all morning—not real tests—those psychological things. It was kind of fun."

"How did you do?"

Sarah shrugged. "I don't know. You had to figure out things."

Actually, she thought she'd done pretty well. Lutie and Megan and Heather had talked about little else during their lunch hour, and Sarah had joined in enthusiastically. As long as they talked about the tests, they weren't talking about the Cavemen's concert.

She'd been dreading the moment when she'd have to tell the girls she definitely wouldn't be able to go with them. It had been easier to tell Lutie, alone, on the way home from school. Lutie was disappointed, but she didn't protest at the top of her lungs the way Heather would have, or ask questions about the Prescotts' money problems the way Megan might. Tomorrow Lutie would tell the other girls Sarah wasn't going to the concert, and she'd probably tell them to say as little about it as possible. She was a good friend.

"Lloyd and I have a surprise for you," Mrs. Prescott said, breaking in on Sarah's thoughts. "I tried to get him to stay home until you got here, but he had very important business at Teddy's house. So I'll have to show you myself."

Puzzled, Sarah followed her mother upstairs. When they passed Aunt Margaret's door, Mrs. Prescott waved gaily. "I'm going to show Sarah what we've been up to this afternoon," she said. They continued down the hall to the closed door of Sarah's room.

"Are you ready?"

Sarah nodded.

Triumphantly, Mrs. Prescott threw open the door. "What do you think?" she demanded, and stepped back so Sarah could look inside.

The boxes were gone. There had been at least a dozen of them stacked against the walls and under the windows, almost hiding the handsome hardwood floor. The old sewing machine was gone, too.

"Lloyd and I carried everything up to the attic as soon as he came home from school," Mrs. Prescott said proudly. "And Aunt Margaret cheered us on. Doesn't it look different?" She watched Sarah anxiously.

"It looks great," Sarah said. "It really does, Mom." She tried to match her tone to her mother's.

"We both decided we'd like to contribute something," Mrs. Prescott said, pointing to the braided rugs that covered the spaces where the boxes had stood. "One's from Lloyd's room and the other's from ours. And l found the curtains in one of the boxes. l promised l'd make you some when l had time, but these are nicer than any l could put together. l like ruffles in a bedroom."

"They're really pretty," Sarah agreed. "And thanks for the rugs."

"You can thank Lloyd yourself later." Mrs. Prescott leaned across the bed to straighten one of the old-fashioned flower prints she'd hung on the wall. "That big painting is in the back of your closet," she went on in a louder voice. "Your dad can hang it if you want him to—that's up to you."

"l'm not sure," Sarah said.

"Or maybe instead of the painting you'd like a bulletin board," Mrs. Prescott suggested. "There're some pieces of wallboard in the basement—l'm sure Dad could fix up something for snapshots and souvenirs."

Sarah shifted from one foot to the other, aware of how one-sided this conversation must sound to Aunt Margaret in her room down the hall. *l bet she thinks l'm a spoiled kid who doesn't appreciate what my mother does for me. But l do. l really do!* It wasn't her mother's fault that the shining, freshly curtained little room still felt like a storeroom to her. It wasn't her mother's fault, or her father's, or even Aunt Margaret's that her life had changed. *l know that,* she thought irritably, *but knowing doesn't help!* The changes might be easier to accept if there were someone to blame.

She gave her mother a hug. "The bulletin board's a neat idea." she said. "I'll ask Dad to make one this weekend—if he has time."

At dinner that night everyone was acutely aware of Mr. Prescott's empty chair. They ate quickly, and afterward Mrs. Prescott announced that she and Lloyd were going to the library for an hour or so.

"Not again," Lloyd groaned. "I want to watch television."

"It's okay with me if he stays home," Sarah said quickly. She dreaded another evening alone.

But her mother was firm. "You have Aunt Margaret to take care of and your homework to do," she said. "That's enough responsibility. Lloyd, we'll find you a good book in the children's section. It's about time you realized reading can be fun."

"Fun!" Lloyd grumbled. "Like carrying all those boxes to the attic was fun." He cast a martyred look in Sarah's direction. "How come I'm old enough to carry boxes but not old enough to look after myself?"

"Put on your boots," Mrs. Prescott said. "The sooner we go the sooner we'll be back."

As soon as they left, Sarah went through the downstairs, turning on extra lights. She peered into the storage closet—all quiet—and pushed back the clothes in the front hall closet so there were no hidden places where someone—or something—could lurk. Then she settled down in her usual corner of the couch with her math and history books beside her. She had promised to check on Aunt Margaret every half hour, but her mother thought it likely the old lady would sleep all evening. She was tired after sitting up in her wheelchair most of the afternoon.

Math first, Sarah decided. She picked up her notebook and started working out a problem. It was a difficult one. *If only Lutie were here,* she thought, *we could work together and finish in half the time.* And if Lutie were sitting beside her, she wouldn't have this sickish feeling that something bad was about to happen. Lutie thought living in a possibly haunted house would be exciting.

Sarah wasn't sure when she began to feel cold. At first she tried to convince herself that it was her imagination; she could hear the furnace clicking on and off in its regular pattern. But the chill deepened. She pulled the afghan from the back of the couch and wrapped it around her shoulders. She should probably go upstairs to see if Aunt Margaret wanted extra covers.

She unfolded her cramped legs and stood up. She was shivering now, and it wasn't just because of the temperature of the room. This was what had happened that other time: first the unexplainable chill, and then. . . .

"Gabe? Where are you?"

A heart-stopping burst of activity in the narrow space behind the sofa answered her question. Gabe had been napping in one of his favorite hideaways, and she had awakened him. Out he came, stretching and yawning, and Sarah bent to pat him just as a creaking sound began overhead.

Gabe cocked his head and began to growl. *Not again!* She watched the dog move, stiff-legged, across the living room and front hall to the foot of the stairs. Hardly breathing, Sarah followed him. They stood side by side, staring upward, listening to the march of slow footsteps overhead.

I can't call the police again! They'll laugh at me. . . . The steps were approaching Aunt Margaret's door now. Perhaps she heard them and was too frightened to cry out. Sarah thought about what that would be like—to lie helpless in bed, unable to move, waiting, waiting. . . .

"Come *on*, Gabe!" She tried to push the big dog ahead of her, but he whimpered and hung back. Growling at an intruder was one thing; going to find him was clearly something else. Sarah grabbed his collar and dragged him behind her up the stairs.

Halfway to the top, she stopped and listened.

The footsteps had stopped, too; whoever it was must be close to Aunt Margaret's door. Sarah's knees trembled so violently she could hardly stand.

"Sarah? Is that you in the hall?" Aunt Margaret's voice sounded sleepy and confused.

Sarah forced herself up another step, then stopped again. Someone was singing! High and flutelike, the voice drifted through the air!

"Thou wilt come no more, gentle Annie,
Like a flower thy spirit did depart.
Thou are gone, alas! like the many
That have bloomed in the summer of my
 heart."

It was the sweetest voice, and the saddest song, Sarah had ever heard. Who could it be? She leaned against the wall, with Gabe cowering beside her.

"Somebody! Help me!" Aunt Margaret's cry cut off the last notes of the song. With a gasp, Sarah broke from her trance and raced up the rest of the stairs, pulling Gabe with her. The upstairs hall appeared empty, though it was hard to see, since the only light came from Aunt Margaret's doorway. Sarah ran across the room to where her great-aunt huddled under the comforter. Her blue eyes were glazed with terror.

"Who is it?" she cried. "Who's out there?"

Sarah looked over her shoulder. The doorway

was empty. "l—l don't know," she stammered. "l thought l heard—"

"You thought you heard!" Aunt Margaret lowered the comforter slightly. "You *thought* you heard," she repeated in her quavering voice. "Someone was singing out there—no 'thought' about it. Some friend of yours, l suppose. Wandering around the house singing and waking up decent people. Shame on her!"

Sarah stared. The words were accusing, but she realized Aunt Margaret was begging for reassurance. She wanted Sarah to say yes, she did have a friend staying with her for the evening, and yes, the friend had been singing a sad song.

"l'm sorry but there's no one here but us, Aunt Margaret," Sarah said reluctantly. "Maybe we heard someone passing by outside. Somebody playing a radio." It was the only explanation she could think of, and she knew it was a weak one.

They stared at each other for a moment, and Sarah put out her hand. Aunt Margaret hesitated, then slid one hand from under the comforter. Her fingers were very cold.

"You think it was somebody passing by," she said. "With a radio."

Sarah nodded. Of course, the windows were closed, and people seldom went walking for pleasure on a night like this. Still. . . . "Would you like a cup of tea, Aunt Margaret?"

The old lady shook her head. "No tea," she

whispered, her glance flicking nervously toward the door. "People shouldn't play their radios that loud. They should be more thoughtful."

Sarah drew the rocking chair close to the bed and sat down, grateful that she didn't have to go to the kitchen for tea. Gabe leaned against her knees.

"Lloyd has a Chinese checkers board in his room," she said. "Would you like to play for a while?"

"I won't be able to hold the marbles." Again there was that frightened glance toward the door.

"You can point, and I'll move them for you." It seemed important to Sarah that they do something, anything but talk about what had just happened.

"I guess I'd rather just try to go back to sleep," Aunt Margaret said. "That song . . . it reminded me. . ." She shook her head against the pillow. "Will you stay here till I fall asleep?"

Sarah felt as if she'd stepped over an invisible line and was suddenly much older than she'd been a few minutes before. "I'll be right here," she said. "Don't worry."

Her great-aunt gave her a long look and closed her eyes. The look said a lot. It said she was willing to pretend the song they'd heard had come from a passing radio, even though they both knew that wasn't true. It was a look that said, very clearly, *I need you.*

Sarah turned the rocking chair to face the door. She felt suddenly, fiercely protective. *Go to sleep,* she urged Aunt Margaret. *I'm here.*

If the footsteps and the singing started again, she didn't want her great-aunt to hear them.

Ten

IT SEEMED LIKE HOURS, but actually only twenty minutes passed before Sarah heard Lloyd stamping snow from his boots in the back hall and complaining that he'd missed his favorite program. During those twenty minutes she had barely moved; her eyes ached from staring at the empty doorway. Aunt Margaret had seemed to doze, but there was something about the set of her jaw that made Sarah believe she was awake and listening.

"Aunt Margaret, Mom's home. I'm going downstairs. Is that all right?" The blue-veined eyelids fluttered, and Sarah tiptoed across the room.

Her mother and brother were in the kitchen, their cheeks and noses rosy with cold. "Lloyd found a great book of dog stories," Mrs. Prescott announced with determined cheerfulness. "How did you and Aunt Margaret get along?"

Sarah gripped the back of a kitchen chair.

"Something happened, Mom."

Mrs. Prescott looked at her sharply. "What do you mean, something happened? Sarah, if this is going to be more tapping in closets and mysterious footsteps—" She stopped, appalled. "You didn't call the police again, did you?"

"No, I didn't!" Sarah felt her face grow hot. "But I wanted to. I did hear those footsteps again. I *heard* them, Mom. And that's not all." She leaned forward, trying to ignore her mother's expression.

"Wow!" Lloyd exclaimed. "What else?"

"Somebody was singing upstairs. A girl." Sarah kept her eyes on her mother's face, willing her to believe. "Aunt Margaret heard her, too."

Mrs. Prescott's lips tightened. "Lloyd, Sarah and I have to talk. You've been pouting all evening because you wanted to watch television, so go and watch. Now."

"But this is more interesting," Lloyd protested. "I'd rather listen. If the house is haunted I ought to know about it. I live here, too, and I—"

"I said go," Mrs. Prescott repeated. "This minute!"

Muttering under his breath, Lloyd left them. Sarah and her mother stared at each other across the kitchen table.

"Just let me tell you what happened," Sarah pleaded. "I was sitting in the living room doing my homework, when the house started to get cold. Cold as—cold as a tomb."

"When were you in a tomb?" Mrs. Prescott asked sarcastically. "Don't be melodramatic. This house is as warm as can be."

Sarah paused. Her mother was right. When had that dank chill faded? Probably while she'd been sitting next to Aunt Margaret's bed, praying that the footsteps and the singing would not begin again.

"But it *was* cold," Sarah insisted. "And then I heard someone walking very slowly in the upstairs hall, and then I heard singing. . . ."

Mrs. Prescott gestured impatiently. "Did you tell Aunt Margaret this story you're telling me?"

"I didn't have to tell her. I went upstairs, and she said she'd heard the singing, too. She wanted to know if it was a friend of mine, but I could tell she was scared. I said it was probably somebody passing by outside with a radio turned up loud."

Mrs. Prescott looked relieved. "Well, *that* was sensible. Probably accurate, too."

"It wasn't a radio, Mom. It really wasn't! Somebody was singing right here in our house."

Mrs. Prescott pulled out a chair and sat down. "You have to stop this, Sarah," she said. "We've lived here for six months, and you've never let your imagination run wild before. I don't understand why you're so concerned about ghosts and that sort of nonsense now, but I've told you this before and I'll tell you again—" She paused, rubbing her forehead. "If you don't stop, you're going to be very sorry. Aunt Margaret is reasonably happy here, I think—as happy as a person can be when she's helpless and in pain. But if you make her tense and fearful, her condition will get worse. She might even have to go back to Menlo Manor. . . ."

"But I'm not making her afraid," Sarah protested. "It isn't my fault. Ask her yourself."

"I'll do no such thing!" Mrs. Prescott sounded exasperated. "You aren't listening to me. I don't want her to hear any more about this than she already has. And I don't want you bothering your dad with it either. He has enough on his mind. Is that clear?"

Sarah nodded, defeated by her mother's anger. "What about me?" she asked plaintively. "I'm scared, but nobody cares about that."

Mrs. Prescott's expression softened. "I do care," she said. "Of course I do. But in this case you're frightening yourself, Sarah. Maybe not deliberately, but I can't let you upset the whole family."

The silvery tinkle of Aunt Margaret's bell ended the conversation.

"I'll go up," Mrs. Prescott said. "You stay here and think about what I've said."

A moment later Lloyd tiptoed down the hall, peeking over his shoulder to make sure their mother was out of earshot.

"What happened?" he demanded. "Come on, Sarah, tell."

Sarah shook her head. "I can't. I'm not supposed to talk about it."

"But that's not fair," he complained. "I've got a right to know. I need to be ready, so if the same thing happens to me—"

"It won't," Sarah told him. "The only time things happen is when Aunt Margaret and I are home alone."

It was true, if you didn't count that first night when Gabe had barked at something only he had heard. Since then, she and Aunt Margaret had been singled out in a terrifying way.

Later, on her way to bed, Sarah hesitated at her great-aunt's door. The room was dark except for a tiny night-light and the moonbeams that streamed through the windows. She was about to go on, when Aunt Margaret's voice came out of the darkness.

"Goodnight, Sarah. Thank you for staying with me this evening."

"That's okay." Sarah waited. "Have a good sleep."

"I will." Aunt Margaret said it as if she were giving herself an order. "I don't know what got into me tonight. There was no reason to get so upset because someone was playing his radio too loudly. That was very silly of me."

Sarah sighed and said goodnight, feeling more

alone than ever. As she undressed and climbed into bed, she thought about how complicated it was to be part of a family. She'd had an experience that she wanted desperately to share with her mother, but her mother wouldn't listen. Lloyd wanted to hear about it, but she wasn't supposed to tell him. Her father didn't know about it, and she wasn't supposed to tell him, either. And Aunt Margaret, who had been there and *knew*—Aunt Margaret was going to pretend it hadn't happened.

Eleven

PROBABLY NOTHING WILL HAPPEN as long as you're here," Sarah said. "So then you won't believe me either."

She and Lutie sat at the kitchen table, their homework spread between them. Lutie helped herself to a handful of popcorn and glanced quickly over her shoulder. "I'll believe you, anyway." She giggled nervously. "You don't have to show me a ghost, Sarah. I mean, I *thought* I'd like to see one, but now that I'm here—well, I guess I'd rather skip it."

Sarah wanted to skip it, too. When her mother said she and Lloyd would have to deliver one typing assignment and pick up another this evening Sarah had panicked. Then, like an answer to a prayer, Lutie called. Her father was going to a meeting and would drop her off for an hour if the girls wanted to study together.

"Terrific!" Sarah's voice had risen in a squeal of pleasure that made Lloyd roll his eyes.

Mrs. Prescott waited at the kitchen door until the telephone conversation had ended. "Just be careful that you don't disturb Aunt Margaret," she warned. "And get your homework done, won't you?" Sarah heard the unspoken warning: *No silly talk about ghosts.*

"We'll work here in the kitchen," Sarah promised. "I'll make popcorn." *It'll be an ordinary evening. If something happens, it won't be my fault.*

Now Lutie peeked over her shoulder again. "What'll we work on first?" she wondered. "The math's the hardest."

Sarah took out her math text and notebook. "I wish you lived next door instead of five blocks away," she said wistfully. "We could study together every night. Wouldn't that be great?"

"Great!" Lutie opened her text and closed it again. "Do you think we should go upstairs and make sure your aunt is okay before we start?"

Sarah hesitated. The television murmured distantly overhead. She knew Lutie was eager to meet the old lady who had become such an important part of the Prescott household, but there was no hurry. It was so peaceful sitting at the kitchen table. *An ordinary evening.*

"She'll ring if she wants anything," Sarah said. "My mom checked on her just before they left."

For forty minutes the girls struggled with the math, then moved on to the English assignment. There were four poems to be read and a paragraph to be written about each one.

"Let's take turns reading them out loud," Lutie suggested. "I can understand better if I hear the words." She opened the text to the section on Edgar Allan Poe and began:

"It was many and many a year ago,
In a kingdom by the sea,
That a maiden there lived whom you may
   know
By the name of Annabel Lee—

What's the matter, Sarah? Did you hear a noise?"

Sarah shivered. "No, but you just reminded me of something," she said. "The song Aunt Margaret and I heard the other night—the words were something about 'gentle Annie.' Not Annabel—Annie. It had such a sad sound, like this poem."

Lutie cleared her throat. "Maybe I should read another one first."

Before Sarah could reply, a door slammed upstairs with a crash like a thunderclap. Gabe hurtled out from under the table, banging his head on the way, and Lutie gave a little scream.

"What's that?"

Faintly, as if it were very far away, Aunt Margaret's bell began ringing.

"Come on!" Sarah gasped. "Something's wrong!" *This isn't supposed to happen,* she thought. *Not when someone else is here.*

The girls raced down the hall and up the stairs. Aunt Margaret's bedroom door was tightly closed, and behind it the bell rang frantically.

"Maybe we should call someone," Lutie whispered. "What if—"

But Sarah pictured Aunt Margaret, so tiny and helpless in the big bed. She threw open the door and plunged inside.

The room was alive with flickering shadows cast by the fire. Aunt Margaret sat up in bed, the bell clutched in her hand.

"Oh, Sarah," she cried. "I was so frightened—" She saw Lutie standing at the door and her face changed. "You have company."

"This is my best friend Lutie Marks, Aunt Margaret," Sarah said. "What's wrong? What made the door slam like that?"

Aunt Margaret dropped the bell on the bedside table and leaned back on her pillows. She was very pale. "It was a draft, I suppose," she said carefully, looking from Sarah to Lutie. "Someone must have left a window open."

Still pretending, Sarah thought. "We'll check," she said, trying to match Aunt Margaret's casual tone.

Together the girls went into the master bedroom, then to Lloyd's room, and finally to Sarah's. All the windows were closed.

"Your room looks really neat," Lutie said. But she glanced around uneasily as she said it.

Aunt Margaret was waiting for them when they returned. "There *was* an open window, wasn't there?" she said. "I can't understand why anyone would leave a window open on a cold December night. My bones are aching horribly."

"Do you want a pain pill?" Sarah asked, eager to change the subject.

"I certainly do. And please see what's wrong with the television. When the door slammed, the picture disappeared right in the middle of my favorite nature show."

Sarah filled a glass with water from the pitcher on the bedside table, while Lutie fiddled with the television control.

"It's okay now," Lutie reported. She smiled at Aunt Margaret and was rewarded with a stiff little nod.

"Thank you very much. Where's my pill, Sarah?"

Sarah was staring at the little tray on the bedside table. Heart pills, blood pressure pills, arthritis pills—but no pain pills. The squat white bottle was missing.

"It—it isn't here," she stammered.

"Of course it's there!" The sharp retort held a ring of fear.

"I'll find it," Sarah said. "On the dresser, or

maybe. . ." But there was no bottle in sight. The medicines were always kept in the same place, within easy reach when they were needed.

"Look on the mantel," Aunt Margaret said, her voice tight. Sarah knew she was remembering where they'd found the missing bell.

While Lutie and Aunt Margaret watched, Sarah moved along the mantel, lifting pictures or peering behind them. Her hands shook, and she realized she was holding her breath.

The missing bottle was inside a small blue vase that had belonged to Aunt Margaret's mother. Sarah took it out, opened it, and removed a pill. She put the pill in a cup and handed it and the water glass to Aunt Margaret without meeting the old lady's eyes.

The doorbell rang, making them all jump.

"That must be my dad!" Lutie exclaimed. She sounded relieved. "I'll have to go, Sarah."

Sarah didn't blame her for wanting to leave. "I'll be right back," she promised Aunt Margaret and followed her friend to the top of the stairs.

Mr. Marks, having made his presence known, had returned to the car to wait. "Are you going to be okay?" Lutie whispered. "I wish your mother would come home."

"We'll be fine," Sarah told her with more confidence than she felt. "Don't forget your books."

Lutie looked at Sarah earnestly. "It was probably just a draft," she said. "Old houses have drafts, even when the windows are closed. And your mom must have put the pills in that vase—to keep them safe."

The girls stared at each other, and Sarah realized how much could be said without words. *I'm sorry for you, Sarah,* Lutie seemed to be saying. *I thought it would be fun to have a ghost in the house, but I guess I'd rather hear about it than be here when it comes.*

When Sarah returned to the bedroom, the chill was gone and the television was playing softly. Her great-aunt lay on her side watching the door.

"Are you feeling better, Aunt Margaret?"

The old lady nodded. "Much better. I don't think we need to say anything to your mother about finding the pills in the vase. I don't want to get anyone in trouble."

Sarah was startled. "I didn't put them there," she said. "Is that what you think?"

"No, I don't. But your mother will want a logical explanation, and I just can't think of one. So why trouble her?"

Sarah thought it over. The suddenly slammed door wouldn't impress her mother one bit, and if she was told about the missing pills, she'd insist that either Sarah or Lloyd had been playing tricks with Aunt Margaret's belongings. Again.

"I guess you're right." She smiled shakily, and Aunt Margaret smiled back.

"When I talk about not getting anyone in trouble, I'm thinking of myself, too, Sarah. People are quick to believe that when a person gets old she begins to think fuzzily and imagine things. Well, let me tell you"— the blues eyes sparked—"there is nothing wrong with my mind. I don't imagine things, and I don't want your parents to think I'm starting to—to crack up."

The slang phrase sounded strange coming from Aunt Margaret, but Sarah knew that was exactly what her mother *would* think.

"We have a problem," Aunt Margaret continued. "I have to admit that much. But it isn't something your parents can help us with. I don't like to suggest you keep secrets from them, but in this case. . . . You do understand, don't you?"

Sarah understood. She and her great-aunt were the only members of the family who knew something strange and unnatural was happening in their house. Lutie wanted to believe it, but she didn't live here, and after tonight she probably wouldn't want to come back.

Aunt Margaret and I are partners, Sarah thought wonderingly. It was not the way she'd ever expected to feel about the person who had stolen her bedroom.

Twelve

Lutie was waiting at Sarah's locker the next morning.

"Did anything else happen after I left?" she wanted to know. "I couldn't sleep last night thinking about it all—the door slamming by itself and the pills disappearing. It was weird!"

Sarah tossed her scarf on the locker shelf and dug through her purse for a comb. "Nothing else happened," she said. "Did you finish the English assignment?"

Lutie looked relieved and a little disappointed at the same time. "I don't blame you for being scared," she said, and waited. But Sarah didn't respond. She knew Lutie was sorry for her, and it wasn't a pleasant thought. They were still best friends, but Sarah didn't want to talk about ghosts anymore.

"What are you going to do tonight?" Lutie

asked when they met again at the end of the day.
"Will your mom be at home? I hope so."

"It's my dad's night off so they're going grocery
shopping," Sarah replied. "I'm going to stay
upstairs with Aunt Margaret while they're gone.
We'll keep each other company."

Lutie looked unconvinced, but Sarah had decided that sitting with Aunt Margaret would be
easier than staying downstairs alone. She and her
great-aunt could be nervous together, without
trying to hide their feelings.

Mrs. Prescott looked pleased when Sarah said
she and Aunt Margaret were going to play Chinese
checkers after dinner. "That's a good idea," she
said. "Aunt Margaret has acted a little fretful
today. I'm sure she'll welcome your company. But
what about your homework?"

"I'll do it when you get home from the store."

As soon as her family left, Sarah hurried upstairs and found the Chinese checkers board on
Lloyd's shelf. Aunt Margaret was sitting up in bed,
with a grim expression that softened when Sarah
came in.

"I haven't played a game in years," she said
agreeably. "You'll have to teach me."

"I'll sit on the edge of the bed," Sarah suggested. "And the board can be right next to you.
Will that be all right?"

Aunt Margaret nodded. "Before we start," she
said casually, "please close the door, Sarah. In

case of drafts. And put the shepherd back where he belongs."

Sarah turned, startled, to look at the dresser. The porcelain shepherd was close to the edge.

"I would have asked your mother to move it," Aunt Margaret said, her eyes on the game board, "but it was where it belonged when she was here, a little while ago." She picked up a marble and put it in place with the others of the same color. "I'm going to try to do this myself," she said. "My fingers don't work very well, but perhaps it will be good exercise for them."

"We have lots of time." Sarah tried not to look over her shoulder at the shepherd. If Aunt Margaret could pretend to be calm, she could pretend, too.

"Of course it's harder when the room is cold," Aunt Margaret continued. "Much harder."

Sarah had been trying to ignore the rapidly deepening chill. The door was closed, and the fire in the fireplace sent out a suggestion of warmth, but it wasn't enough to keep back the cold.

They were halfway through the game when the bedside lamp went out. Aunt Margaret gave a little cry and dropped the marble she was holding. Her thin fingers gripped Sarah's wrist.

"What's wrong?"

"I—I don't know." Sarah flicked the lamp switch, but nothing happened. She found her way to the wall switch, and that didn't work either. "I guess a fuse has blown. I know how to change it—my dad showed me—but—"

"But what?"

"The fuse box is in the basement." Sarah went back to the bed and sat down close to Aunt Margaret. "I don't want to go down there in the dark!"

"I wouldn't either," Aunt Margaret said promptly. "We'll just sit here in the firelight till the family comes home. Won't hurt us a bit."

Sarah wondered what she would have done if Aunt Margaret had insisted that the fuse be changed. "We can't play checkers though," she pointed out. "It's too dark to see the color of the marbles."

"Doesn't matter."

Sarah could hear her heart pounding in the silence. She kept stealing glances at the shepherd on the dresser, to see if he was still where she'd put him. In the flickering half-light it was easy to imagine he'd moved.

What would her mother do if she were home? She'd march right down to the basement, of course, and fix the fuse.

What else might she do? Suddenly Sarah remembered an old chimney lamp and a bottle of oil on a shelf in the back of her bedroom closet. Her mother had pointed them out when they were hanging up Sarah's clothes and had commented that the lamp could be useful in an emergency.

"There's an oil lamp in my closet, Aunt Margaret," she said. "I'll get it."

The old lady's fingers tightened on Sarah's wrist. "Better not," she said. "Let's just wait."

Sarah hesitated. She looked again at the figurine on the dresser. "It would be so much easier to wait if we had the lamp," she insisted. "I—I keep imagining things."

Aunt Margaret's grasp loosened. "If you want to then," she said reluctantly. "But hurry. I'd rather you stayed here."

Sarah tiptoed across the room and opened the door. The hall was dark and forbidding.

"Hurry, Sarah," Aunt Margaret urged. "Go as fast as you can. Don't think."

It was good advice. Sarah pictured the lamp and the bottle of oil side by side on the closet shelf, and then she flew down the hall toward her goal. *Don't think about what could be lurking in the dark. Don't listen for tapping in the walls—or footsteps—or a voice singing. Run!*

It was all right until she plunged into the closet. In her haste, she forgot about the forest painting, until a painful crack on the knee reminded her it was there. She moaned as she dragged the painting out to the bedroom, then felt her way back into the closet.

"Sarah, what's wrong?" Aunt Margaret's voice was shrill. "Are you hurt?"

"I'm all right." The lamp and the oil were where

she remembered them. With a little sob of relief, Sarah clutched them against her chest and hurried down the hall toward the glimmering light from the front bedroom.

"What happened? l heard you groan." Aunt Margaret's teeth were actually chattering. The room had grown even colder in the minute or two Sarah had been away from it.

"l bumped into something." She set the lamp on the bedside table and opened the bottle of oil. "Do you know how to make this work?"

"Of course." The old lady's glance darted around the room. "We used these lamps all the time when l was a child. Take off the glass chimney—that's right—and unscrew the bottom part that holds the wick. Pour some oil into the base. Now put the wick back on—oh, dear, matches! What shall we do?"

There was a box of matches in the wood basket on the hearth. Sarah lit the wick and set the chimney back in place. The flame shot up, but when she followed Aunt Margaret's directions and adjusted the wick, it began to burn with a strong, steady light.

"That's better." Sarah felt proud of herself, but when she looked at Aunt Margaret in the lamplight, she was shocked. The old lady's face was sickly pale and pinched with fright.

"M-My shawl."

Sarah dashed to the dresser and pulled open

the bottom drawer. As she bent to find the shawl, she almost bumped her head on something on the dresser top. It was the porcelain shepherd, once more balanced perilously on the edge. She straightened quickly and pushed the figurine back.

"I could hear it moving," Aunt Margaret whispered. "In the dark. While you were gone."

Sarah was dizzy with fright. She sank down on the bed and rolled up her pants leg to examine her knee.

"Oh, Sarah, you're bleeding!"

"It's nothing." She explained about the painting stored in her closet, but while she talked she was listening, with growing desperation, for the sound of a car in the driveway. Her parents had to come home now—*this minute*—before something else happened! Before the oil lamp went out. Before footsteps sounded in the hall. Before—

"What painting are you talking about?" Aunt Margaret interrupted. "Tell me what it looks like."

"It's a little clearing in a woods with a path running through it. The painting was in the storeroom when we moved in. I really liked it—at first."

Aunt Margaret's glance darted around the room, from the door to the shepherd figurine to the bedside table. She reminded Sarah of a small bird watching for cats.

"I want to see it," she said. "I must see it right away. You can take the lamp, Sarah."

"Oh, Aunt Margaret." Sarah didn't think she could bear to make that journey down the hall again. Then a car door slammed below the bedroom window, and she realized they were no longer alone.

"Mom and Dad are home—" she began, but Aunt Margaret brushed the words aside.

"I must see that painting tonight," she repeated. "I won't sleep a wink if I don't. *Please,* take the lamp and get the painting, Sarah. I'll just have a quick look, and then you can put it back."

Downstairs there was much stamping of feet, then exclamations as the Prescotts discovered they couldn't turn on the kitchen light. Sarah picked up the lamp and went to the top of the stairs.

"Some fuses burned out," she shouted.

"You don't say!" She could hear her father chuckling as he went down the basement stairs.

"Are you and Aunt Margaret all right, Sarah?" Her mother sounded nervous.

"Any ghosts up there?" That was Lloyd.

"We're okay. Glad you're home." *More glad than you know,* she added to herself. The chill was already fading from the air, as if her mother and father and Lloyd had brought warmth with them.

She moved swiftly down the hall, holding the lamp high. The painting was where she'd left it, leaning against the bed. She picked it up and started back to Aunt Margaret's room. When she was halfway there, the lights went on.

"Well, that's a relief, isn't it!" Aunt Margaret tried to smile as she watched Sarah prop the painting against the rocking chair and step back.

It's changed again, Sarah thought. *I'm not imagining it.* The green forest glen had become still darker, and on the right side, where giant trees met in a canopy over the path, there was the suggestion of a figure. She blinked and looked again. The figure was so faint, so far back in the shadows, she couldn't be sure it was there at all.

Aunt Margaret stared at the painting as if hypnotized. "It looks different—not exactly the way I remember it." She seemed to be holding herself together, as if the slightest movement might be dangerous. Sarah heard her mother start up the stairs.

"This can't be happening," Aunt Margaret said suddenly. "I don't believe it." She pulled the comforter around her so that the checkers board tilted and marbles spilled over the comforter. Then, as Sarah's mother appeared in the doorway, her voice dropped to a whisper.

"It's all my fault," she said. "I'll have to get out of this house as soon as possible."

Thirteen

WHEN SARAH PASSED the bedroom door the next morning, her mother was lifting Aunt Margaret from the bed to her wheelchair. The painting was nowhere in sight.

"You'll feel better after you've had your breakfast." Mrs. Prescott sounded unhappy. "We'll talk about it later, Aunt Margaret."

Sarah hurried downstairs. *Talk about what?* she wondered, but she was pretty sure she knew the answer. Her mother's tone had been ominous.

A few minutes later Mrs. Prescott came into the kitchen and sat down at the table with a heavy sigh.

"You look tired, hon," Sarah's father said sympathetically. "The patient giving you a hard time this morning?"

"Worse than that."

"Want me to pour you some coffee?"

"Later." Mrs. Prescott folded her hands in front of her. "Aunt Margaret wants to go back to Menlo Manor," she announced. "I'm not sure why. First she said I was working too hard. And then she said things aren't working out here—whatever that means."

Mr. Prescott snorted angrily. "That's ridiculous! She can't complain about the care she's getting. No one could be a better nurse than you are."

"It isn't that. At least, I don't *think* it is. She absolutely refuses to be specific." Sarah realized her mother was close to tears.

"I bet she got scared last night when the lights went out," Lloyd offered. "Maybe she's afraid of the dark." He looked as if he were going to say more, but Mrs. Prescott silenced him with a look.

"Well, *was* there a problem last night, Sarah?" her father asked. "Did Aunt Margaret seem especially upset about the lights?"

Sarah looked down at her cereal bowl. "Sort of. I guess."

"What do you mean, *sort of*?" Mrs. Prescott demanded. "She was very quiet when we got home, but I thought she was just tired. You'd better tell us exactly what happened."

Sarah bit her lip. "We were playing Chinese checkers," she said. "The lights went out, and I went to get the oil lamp from my closet. When I got back—" she saw again her great-aunt's terrified expression, saw the porcelain shepherd teetering at the edge of the dresser— "When I got back, she acted scared."

"Well, you couldn't have been gone more than a minute or two," Mr. Prescott said. "I don't see why she was concerned."

"What else happened?" Sarah thought her mother sounded like a detective. She squirmed uneasily.

"I bumped my knee on the painting in the closet. And when I mentioned it to Aunt Margaret she said she wanted to see the painting. She looked at it, and—and I think it reminded her of something bad. She looked scared, and then she said she was going away."

"Well, I don't understand." Sarah's father leaned back in his chair, looking puzzled. "If it's the painting I'm thinking of, it's harmless enough. Nothing to get upset about."

"Let's go upstairs and ask her," Lloyd suggested. "Maybe there's a curse on the picture—"

"Lloyd David Prescott!" Mrs. Prescott's voice cracked with anger. "You will not say one word to Aunt Margaret about that painting. I've put it away in our closet—there's more room in there. If seeing it brought back unhappy memories for her, I'm sorry, but it's gone now, and she won't have to look at it again. Sarah, is there anything *else* we should hear about last night?"

Sarah shook her head. She knew what would happen if she tried to tell her family that the shepherd figurine had moved around the dresser top by itself. That the bedroom had turned cold. Lloyd would be thrilled, and her mother and father would be disgusted with her. They'd be sure that Aunt Margaret's decision to leave was all Sarah's fault. Her "nonsense" about ghosts had sent the old lady into a panic.

"Well, then," Mrs. Prescott said slowly, "I want you to listen to me carefully. You, too, Lloyd. I hope we can change Aunt Margaret's mind about leaving—and not just because if she goes, we have to go, too. The fact is, she has more right to be here than we have. It's her house. She grew up here. It's up to us to make life pleasant for her now—if it isn't too late!"

"I didn't do anything!" Sarah protested, and for a moment all her resentment of Aunt Margaret came rushing back. "Why is it my fault she wants to leave? Maybe she just doesn't like us."

"Sarah!" her father warned.

"I didn't say it's your fault," Mrs. Prescott said. "You thought fast last night when you got the lamp from your closet. I'm not sure I'd have remembered it if I'd been here alone with Aunt Margaret. But we all have to be careful. If looking at an old painting could upset her that much. . . ." She shrugged. "Elderly people get confused sometimes. We don't know what's going on in Aunt Margaret's mind."

Sarah felt her anger drain away. Poor Aunt

Margaret! She'd been right when she said people were always ready to assume an old person wasn't thinking clearly. She'd been wise to say "things just aren't working out" rather than to admit she was sure the house was haunted.

As soon as she'd finished her cereal and toast, Sarah went back upstairs. Aunt Margaret was sitting near the window, looking at her tray of scrambled eggs, toast, and juice without interest. She greeted Sarah with a troubled smile.

"Good morning. I suppose Ruth told you I'm moving back to the nursing home."

Sarah nodded. "Is it because of last night, Aunt Margaret? I'm sorry I showed you the painting if it made you feel bad. I'm not supposed to talk about that but—"

"I'm leaving because taking care of me is too much for your mother," the old lady said crisply. "She'll deny it, of course, but I know better. The lifting and the running up and down stairs all day—it's too much."

So now Aunt Margaret had decided not to admit the truth to anyone, even Sarah. "But Mom doesn't mind," she argued. "And she doesn't believe that's the reason you want to leave. She thinks—"

"She thinks I'm a silly, befuddled old lady who doesn't know when she's well off," Aunt Margaret interrupted. "It doesn't matter. I'm going."

"But why?" Sarah persisted. "Last night you said 'It's all my fault.' What did you mean?"

"Didn't mean anything," Aunt Margaret shrugged. "Did you tell your mother l said that?"

"No." Sarah paused. "And l didn't say anything about the shepherd moving around. Or the cold. Or the way that painting has changed since the first time l looked at it. lt really has—but Mom and Dad wouldn't believe me."

Aunt Margaret nodded. "So you know how it feels to be doubted," she said. "You'd better go to school now, Sarah. You're going to be late. You can take this tray downstairs with you."

Sarah wanted to ask more questions, but Aunt Margaret leaned back in her chair and closed her eyes. "l'm going to take a nap," she said. "l didn't get much sleep last night, what with one thing and another."

Sarah picked up the tray. How was she going to keep her mind on schoolwork today? she wondered.

"Sarah?" Aunt Margaret's voice stopped her at the door. "Did anything supernatural ever happen in this house before l came to stay with you?"

Sarah tried to think. "The day before you came, the shepherd figurine fell on the floor," she said slowly. "l don't know if that was supernatural, but l'm pretty sure l didn't put it near the edge of the dresser."

Aunt Margaret nodded and closed her eyes again. "Think about that, Sarah. The shepherd is something l cherish. And ever since then, unexplainable things keep happening. Do you blame me for not wanting to stay around to see what might happen next?"

All that day, Sarah kept hearing Aunt Margaret's words. Her math teacher scolded her for not paying attention, and Lutie asked a half-dozen times what was wrong. "Did the ghost come back last night?" she demanded excitedly. "Did you hear those footsteps again?"

Reluctantly, Sarah told her friend about the lights going out and described how she'd gone down the hall to her bedroom to get the oil lamp. "But it was just burned-out fuses," she said. "My dad fixed them when he got home."

Lutie shivered. "You're *brave,* Sarah. How could you walk through the dark when you might have bumped smack into a ghost?"

"I had to." Sarah wished she could tell Lutie how good it had felt to find that lamp and bring it back. "No big deal," she said, deciding to be modest. But it felt like a very big deal indeed.

Fourteen

CAN IT POSSIBLY WAIT until morning, Professor? My husband will be home then. It's difficult for me to get away in the evening right now." Mrs. Prescott waved at Sarah who was just coming in from school.

I wasn't supposed to hear that, Sarah thought. She dropped her books on the kitchen table and waited for the conversation to end. It was clear from her mother's strained expression that the person she was talking to did *not* want to wait until morning.

Sarah held her breath. These last five nights, with her mother at home, had been wonderfully uneventful. There had been no tapping in the walls, no sudden drops in temperature. The porcelain shepherd and the rest of Aunt Margaret's possessions had stayed where they belonged. And though Aunt Margaret had been cranky and de-

manding, she'd said nothing more about returning
to Menlo Manor.

When Mrs. Prescott hung up the phone, she
was shaking her head.

"That Professor Blake!" she exclaimed. "He's
one of my best customers, but he does let things
go till the very last minute. Now he has to have a
report typed up by day after tomorrow, and he
has classes tomorrow morning, so we can't go
over it then. I'll have to see him tonight. Do you
mind?"

Sarah minded. She wanted to shout "You can't
go!" at the top of her lungs. But her mother looked
tired and depressed. She didn't need any more
problems.

"It's not that I don't trust you Sarah," Mrs.
Prescott said. "I know you don't mean to upset
Aunt Margaret. But when you're here alone you
get nervous, and then she gets nervous, too. It
takes so little to put her in a state!" She shook
her head ruefully. "The coffee is too hot or too
cold, the eggs are too hard, the bedsheets are
tucked in too tightly, the wheelchair squeaks. . . ."
She picked up her coffee cup and stared into it.
"Your father has a theory. He thinks Aunt Margaret doesn't want to go back to Menlo Manor, but
she thinks she should. She really believes I'll wear
myself out taking care of her. I've told her again
and again that's nonsense, but your dad thinks
she's trying to prove she's right. He thinks she

complains about everything so that I *will* give up and tell her to leave. What do you think?''

For a moment Sarah considered telling her mother the truth. *Yes! Aunt Margaret is looking for an excuse to leave. She knows our house is haunted, and she's scared to death. So am I.* But she knew that kind of talk would only make her mother more upset.

"You must be very careful this evening,'' Mrs. Prescott went on. "I know you and Lloyd enjoy the idea of a ghost and that sort of silliness, but a sick old lady isn't going to understand your flights of fancy—or appreciate them!''

Enjoy! Sarah thought indignantly. *Flights of fancy!* What would her mother say if *she* saw the porcelain shepherd moving across the dresser top!

"Anyway, if she's trying to be difficult, I certainly hope she gives it up pretty soon,'' Mrs. Prescott went on. "I'm not going to quit, but it's getting so I dread the sound of that bell.''

As if on signal, the bell rang, jangling and impatient.

"I'll go,'' Sarah offered. "You finish your coffee, Mom. Maybe she'll play Chinese checkers with me.''

"I doubt it.'' Mrs. Prescott said glumly. "She says bending over the game board makes her neck hurt.''

Sarah doubted it, too. She'd suggested playing once or twice since the night the lights went out, and Aunt Margaret had refused. She was cool, almost unfriendly now, her gaze fastened on the television screen when Sarah stopped in to chat.

"I've dropped the television control," she said crossly, as soon as Sarah entered the room. "It's probably broken."

Sarah scooped up the control from under the wheelchair and pressed one button, then another. The channels changed smoothly.

"Well, it *might* have broken," Aunt Margaret grumbled. "Everything else is going wrong these days."

"Do you want to play checkers?"

Aunt Margaret hesitated, then shook her head. "I don't think so. Your mother isn't going out this evening, is she?"

"She has to," Sarah said. "Just for a little while."

"I wish she wouldn't."

"So do I. But she has to."

They stared at each other, and for a moment, at least, the closeness was back. *We're both so scared,* Sarah thought. *And we can't tell anyone, not even each other.*

They weren't the only members of the family who were unhappy about Mrs. Prescott's change of plans. Lloyd complained bitterly when he found out he'd have to accompany his mother to the college.

"This is the best television night of the week,"

he groaned. "I don't see why—"

Mrs. Prescott cut him off impatiently. "You've seen enough television to last you for a while, young man. Anyway, we won't be gone long." She smiled at Sarah over his head as she spoke, softening a note of warning. "Just keep Aunt Margaret as contented as possible, Sarah. She wants to sit up in her wheelchair, so maybe she'll read for a while."

As soon as they were gone, Sarah hurried upstairs. She took her father's big flashlight with her, and she carried the oil lamp from her closet to Aunt Margaret's room. Then she went from room to room turning on lights. There would be no shadowy corners this evening, unless, of course, a fuse burned out again.

When she laid the checkers board on the bedtray and settled the tray across the arms of the wheelchair, Aunt Margaret nodded resignedly.

"Might as well try to keep busy," she said. Her voice trembled, and she wouldn't meet Sarah's eyes.

"Mom won't be gone long," Sarah said. "She promised."

"Trouble can come in a hurry," Aunt Margaret retorted. "Let's just play and not talk."

They were halfway through the first game when the room began to grow cool. Aunt Margaret's gnarled fingers twitched as she hopped a blue marble over a red one.

Sarah glanced at the shepherd figurine. It was where it was supposed to be, at the back of the dresser, but as she looked, a magazine lying on the dresser top flipped open. She gave a little cry of alarm.

"Dear heaven!" Aunt Margaret pointed at her bedside table. The water glass was sliding slowly toward the edge. Sarah dived to catch it, upsetting the checkers board. Marbles flew across the carpet.

Aunt Margaret leaned forward, breathing fast. "Sarah, this is going to be worse than ever. I can tell! I want you to get that painting and bring it here. I have to look at it again!"

Sarah was aghast. "Oh, Aunt Margaret, I can't. Mom would kill me."

A window shade shot upward with a heart-stopping crack. The curtains billowed as if lifted by a wind.

"Get it," Aunt Margaret insisted. "I have to have one more look. Have to be sure . . . *please!*"

Sarah looked around fearfully. If her mother could see what was happening here, she'd never again talk about "flights of fancy."

"The painting's still in Mom's closet, I guess. I'll be right back." She darted across the hall into her parents' brightly lit bedroom. The closet door was partly open and she could see the painting inside, propped against the back wall.

"Sarah, hurry!" Aunt Margaret sounded frantic.

A loud tapping had begun across the hall. It grew louder with each passing second.

Sarah dragged the painting out of the closet and tilted it toward the light.

For a moment she wasn't sure it was the same picture. The forest scene was almost totally dark, with the harsh outlines of tree branches against a clouded sky. The figure, barely visible before, was unmistakable now. A tall man with flaming reddish hair and a square-trimmed beard stood among the trees. His lips were drawn back in a grin that made a flash of white in the darkness.

Sarah gasped, and the painting slipped from her fingers. When she picked it up, the red-haired man was gone.

Did I imagine him? She knew there were trick pictures that changed, depending on how the light struck them, but when she tilted the painting at a different angle the man didn't reappear.

There was a crash from across the hall, and Aunt Margaret screamed. Then the scream changed to a long wail. Sarah dropped the painting and ran.

The scene in Aunt Margaret's bedroom was one she'd relive in nightmares for years to come. The wheelchair was careening around the room like an over-sized windup toy. Its helpless passenger leaned backward, her hands clutching the arms of the chair, her mouth a round O of terror.

"Sarah, help me!"

The chair caromed off the foot of the bed and sideswiped the rocker. Sarah took a step into the room, and at once the chair shot toward her. She leapt back into the hall, and then, as the chair came through the door, she grabbed the arms.

The nightmare worsened. She couldn't stop the chair; she could hardly even slow it. Step by step, it forced her backward toward the top of the stairs.

Aunt Margaret's siren-wail broke off as she saw what must happen next.

"Let go!" she gasped. "Get out of the way, Sarah! You'll fall!"

Sarah stepped backward into space and went down one step, then another, with jarring force. The front wheels of the chair were suspended in air, and Aunt Margaret began to tip forward.

"Hi! I'm home."

Lloyd's cheerful crow from the kitchen was completely unexpected. For what seemed an endless time Sarah stared up into Aunt Margaret's terrified eyes. Then the wheelchair shot back into the hall. The front wheels dropped to the floor with a thump, and Sarah fell forward.

"Hey, what's wrong?" Lloyd stood at the bottom of the stairs, frowning up at them.

Sarah scrambled to her feet, and Aunt Margaret began maneuvering the chair back toward her room.

"Nothing's wrong," Sarah said breathlessly.

She wondered if she was going to be sick. "I practically fell down the stairs, that's all."

"Klutz." Lloyd sat on the bottom step and began tugging at his boots. "I don't feel good," he announced cheerfully. "Mom said I should come home and lie down."

Sarah felt as if her knees were going to give way, but she tried to keep her voice steady. She didn't want to tell Lloyd what had just happened. Her parents would have to know—after all, she and Aunt Margaret might have been killed—but Lloyd was just a little boy.

"Are you really sick," she demanded, "or did you say you were so you could come home and watch television?"

"Both," Lloyd said, sounding pleased with himself. "Mrs. Blake was just going out when we got there, and when she heard me tell Mom my stomach hurt, she offered to bring me back home. I'm not supposed to bother you. Hey, you look weird," he added, grinning up at her. "Weirder than usual."

Sarah managed to make a face—her usual response when he teased. "You look pretty weird yourself," she told him. "Drink some Coke—it'll settle your stomach."

She stayed at the top of the stairs till she heard the television set click on in the living room. Then she hurried in to Aunt Margaret. The old lady had positioned her chair next to the bedside table and was fumbling with one of the bottles. Her face was gray.

"Can't get the cover off," she said hoarsely. "Hurry."

Sarah glanced at the label as she twisted the cover from the bottle. It was the heart medicine. She tipped a single pill into Aunt Margaret's hand and helped her put it under her tongue.

Almost at once, the gray look faded, and a faint pink came back to her great-aunt's cheeks.

"Are you okay now?"

"I don't know," Aunt Margaret rubbed her forehead. "Are you?"

"I don't know either."

"For the last few days I've been hoping I was wrong," Aunt Margaret said shakily. "I've been hoping—I've been hoping it was *you* making these terrible things happen."

"Me!" Sarah could hardly believe her ears.

"I don't mean I thought you deliberately caused them," Aunt Margaret said. "But it occurred to me that perhaps they happened because you're here. You've heard of poltergeists, haven't you? A poltergeist is a mischievous spirit that plays tricks on people. Our *adventures* have always happened when you were here, Sarah—once when you and your friend Lutie were here together. I began to wonder if this particular poltergeist makes itself known to young girls. I've never believed in that sort of thing, but now. . . ."

She rubbed her head again. "That's why I wanted to look at the painting again. I thought it might help me to decide whether the problem was you or me. But now I don't have to see the painting to be sure. After tonight, I know that whatever strange things happen here, they happen because of me."

"Please, Aunt Margaret, let's tell Mom and Dad this time," Sarah begged. "They'll have to believe us! Maybe they'll know what to do."

The old lady shook her head. "I already know what to do. I have to leave. But before I go there's a story I want to tell you, Sarah. It's a true story. I'd rather *not* talk about it, but you deserve to know. And when you do, you'll see for yourself why I have to go. In fact," she added with a wry little smile, "no doubt you'll want to help me pack."

Fifteen

"WHEN I WAS YOUR AGE I was a lot like you, Sarah. I even looked like you." Aunt Margaret pointed at the portrait above the fireplace. "You see, my hair was long and brown and heavy like yours, and my eyebrows were thick and dark. The first time I saw you I remembered—for just a moment—exactly how it felt to be me when I was a child."

I'm not a child, Sarah protested automatically, but she was too tired to argue. She didn't feel like listening to a story, either. She just wanted her mother to come home.

"Your best friend is Lutie, and mine was Anne. Anne Morris." Aunt Margaret's voice was weak but determined. "Anne was a sweet, quiet girl, and she was strong, too. Her father—Jack Morris—was an artist. His name was in the paper occasionally, and once he had a show of his paintings in a gallery downtown. I envied her that—at first. Being an artist's daughter sounded so glamorous. But as we got to know each other better, she told me what life was like at her house. Jack Morris was an evil-tempered, cruel, entirely selfish man. Anne didn't use those words—she didn't have to. It was clear from everything she said that he cared only about himself."

Sarah began to see where Aunt Margaret's story was leading. "Is the forest painting one of his?"

The old lady nodded. "My father bought it soon after Anne and I became friends. He liked it very much, but he also wanted to help Jack Morris.

"Anne and I used to sit in front of this fireplace just the way we're sitting now," Aunt Margaret continued. "We talked about school and about boys and about getting married and wondered how many children we'd have. Sometimes Anne would cry and say she didn't *want* to get married— she didn't want to take a chance on being treated the way her father treated her mother. He drank a lot, and even though he was a talented painter, they never had much money. Anne worried a lot about her mother and about what was going to become of them. Once in a while she stayed here overnight, and we'd talk till nearly dawn. She used to say I was the luckiest person she knew."

The old voice faded and stopped, but for only a moment. "Anne didn't stay with me very often. Mrs. Morris had a bad heart, and she couldn't stand up to her husband when he got mean. Anne could. She was a frail-looking girl, but she never backed down. I think her father was a little afraid of her. . . ."

"So what happened to them? Where's Anne now?"

"One night she stayed here with me, and in the morning her father came to get her. He said her mother had had a heart attack during the night and was in the hospital. They went off together, and that evening Anne called to say her mother had died. She sounded so lost. So alone. I felt—"

"Hey, Sarah, where's the popcorn?" Lloyd's bellow from the foot of the stairs made them both jump. Sarah went out in the hall.

"I thought you didn't feel good." She tried to sound stern, but her heart wasn't in it. She was grateful he was there.

"I'm better. You don't want me to get weak from hunger, do you?"

"Fat chance," Sarah retorted. "The popcorn's on the shelf nearest the stove. Don't eat too much or you really *will* get sick."

She slipped into her mother's bedroom and put the painting into the closet without looking at it. Then she hurried back to the rocker in front of the fireplace. Aunt Margaret seemed a little stronger now. She was sitting up straight in her chair, tapping the arms with impatient fingers.

"I want you to hear this, Sarah," she said. "It's

more important than popcorn. When your mother comes home, there may not be another chance."

"I'm sorry, Aunt Margaret." Sarah pulled the rocker close to the wheelchair.

"After Mrs. Morris died, Anne stayed here quite often. Once her father went on a terrible drinking binge, and she was with us for a whole week. When he finally sobered up and discovered Anne had been with us all the time he was drunk—well, I guess that was what gave him the idea."

"What idea?"

"He came here with Anne one evening. He looked wretched—his clothes were wrinkled and stained as if he hadn't changed for days—and he suggested that Anne come to live with us. He said she was lonely and unhappy without her mother, and he even offered to let my parents adopt her if they wished. He said Anne and I were best friends, and it would be good for us both to have a sister. He said everything except the truth—that he didn't want to be bothered with a daughter anymore."

Sarah tried to imagine what it would feel like to have your father try to give you away. "Poor Anne," she said softly. "Was she there when he said those things?"

Aunt Margaret nodded. "It was terribly humiliating for her. Because he wouldn't stop talking about it, you see. My parents said Anne was welcome to stay with us for a while, but they

weren't ready to talk about adoption. That made
him furious—I guess he thought he could get
everything settled in one night. He kept saying we
had a beautiful home and plenty of money, and
we ought to be willing to share it with someone
who had less. There was a dreadful scene, and
finally my father ordered him out of the house.
My father told Anne she was welcome to stay, but
Jack grabbed her by the wrist and pulled her away
with him. She called good-bye, and that was the
very last time I heard her voice until—"

"Until when?"

Aunt Margaret didn't answer the question. "A
short time after that, we heard that Anne had
been sent to live with some cousins in Atlanta.
She wrote to me once, and I could tell she hated
it there. The cousins already had a big family to
care for, and they didn't want another mouth to
feed. Her letter made me feel so guilty."

"It wasn't your fault her father didn't want
her," Sarah protested. "Why should you feel
guilty?"

"I think it *was* my fault she didn't come to live
with us," Aunt Margaret said. "My parents asked
me how I felt about her coming, and I said I wasn't
sure. I loved Anne, you see, but my brother and
I were quite spoiled. I wanted Anne as a friend,
but I wasn't quite ready to accept her as a sister.
And then it was too late. Six months after she
moved to Atlanta, there was a fire, and Anne and

two of her little cousins died."

"Oh, Aunt Margaret!" Sarah shivered. "How awful!"

"She and I were in the school chorus together," Aunt Margaret said. She reached out to take Sarah's hand. "We sang one song that was said to be Abraham Lincoln's favorite. It was called 'Gentle Annie.' I used to sing it to tease Anne. . . . And now you see why I'm telling you all this, don't you?"

Sarah sat very still. It seemed to her that she could hear that high sweet soprano as clearly as if the singer were in the room with them now:

> *Thou wilt come no more, gentle Annie,*
> *Like a flower thy spirit did depart. . . .*

"But Anne was your friend, Aunt Margaret. If she came back to this house, she wouldn't try to scare you. She'd never try to push your wheelchair down the stairs."

"Of course not," Aunt Margaret agreed. "I was frightened when I heard her singing, but I never thought she'd do us any harm. There's more to the story, though. Jack Morris—"

She broke off as a car door slammed next to the house.

"It's Mom!" Sarah exclaimed. "Tell me fast. What about Jack Morris?"

"He came to our house one more time, right

after Anne was killed. He raged at my father and
mother and at me, too—said Annie would still be
alive if we hadn't been too selfish to give her a
home. I suppose it was his own guilt driving him
to say the terrible things he said. After all, Anne
never would have had to go away at all if he'd
been a loving father. He shouted at us, threw
things, said we were responsible for her living in
a 'firetrap.' He looked at me with such hatred—
furious because I was alive and *his* daughter was
dead. I remember his exact words when my father
tried to make him leave—'Some day you'll be
sorry! That pampered kid of yours is going to
suffer for what you've done to my girl!' Then he
stormed out, and we didn't see him again. A
couple of years later he was killed in a drunken
brawl.''

Sarah could hear her mother talking to Lloyd in
the living room. Scolding him, she guessed, for
pretending to be sick so he could come home
and watch television. And Lloyd was defending
himself. *Keep talking, Lloyd,* she thought. *Just a
couple more minutes. . . .*

''You think they've both come back, don't you,
Aunt Margaret? You think they're haunting us
because you're living here. . . .''

''What else can I think? When you showed me
the painting the other night, it didn't look the way
I remembered it—that's why I wanted to see it
again. If it had really changed, then I'd be sure

Jack Morris had come back." She shuddered. "He was right about one thing. He said, 'You'll be sorry,' and I am. I've been sorry every day of my life that we didn't help Anne when we had the chance."

Sarah heard her mother starting up the stairs. She jumped up and busied herself straightening the pillow behind Aunt Margaret's shoulders. "What did Jack Morris look like?" she whispered.

"He was very handsome," Aunt Margaret replied. "Tall, auburn hair, a beard. He was handsome and he was charming and he was talented, and he was as wicked as they come."

"Who was wicked?" Mrs. Prescott demanded. She looked at them anxiously.

"I've been boring Sarah with my memories," Aunt Margaret said briskly. "Don't bother to deny it, Sarah. I don't blame you a bit." She smiled cheerfully at Mrs. Prescott. "That's another thing that I like about Menlo Manor. My friends and I tell each other stories all day. I listen to theirs and they listen to mine. It works out very nicely. I'm looking forward to getting back there."

Sixteen

THE HOUSE WAS QUIET. Sarah remembered a time when Lloyd had been sick in bed with a dangerously high temperature. They had walked on tiptoe and talked in whispers, as though the slightest sound might make him worse. She felt like whispering now.

"I'm not blaming you, Sarah," Mrs. Prescott said. "I'm just disappointed. I really thought she'd forgotten about leaving, but I was wrong. She's made up her mind, and we have to accept it. I'm to call Menlo Manor this morning to see if they have a room for her."

They were sitting at the kitchen table, eating breakfast, or pretending to. Sarah's cornflakes had long ago turned to mush. Even Lloyd seemed to have lost his appetite.

"What happened?" he demanded. "What got her upset again?"

"Who knows?" Mrs. Prescott shook her head, as if she were tired of thinking. "It doesn't matter, does it? We can't force her to stay if she doesn't want to."

Sarah almost wished her mother would insist on knowing whether anything had happened to disturb Aunt Margaret last night. She felt weighted down by the knowledge that they both could have been badly hurt—even killed—by the runaway wheelchair. But apparently her mother wasn't going to ask. *And what would I tell her, anyway? How could I make her believe in a wheelchair that moved by itself?*

"I s'pose we're going to have to move then," Lloyd said gloomily. "Just when I have a chance to make the soccer team." He eyed his mother. "And just when I'm getting A's in math," he added, in case math might be more important than soccer in deciding whether they would go or stay.

Mrs. Prescott sighed. "As a matter of fact, we probably won't have to leave here," she said. "And in a way I feel worse about that than anything. We've never talked about our finances with Aunt Margaret—I didn't want her to realize how tight things are right now. But it turns out she's been very much aware of it. When I was helping her to bed last night, she said we mustn't worry about the rent—she could get by on half of what we paid before, until your father gets a well-paying job again. She's known we had a problem all along, and even though she doesn't want to live with us, she's worried about how we're going to manage. She really cares—so why does she want to leave? I just don't understand it."

Sarah stood up. "I'll get her breakfast tray before I go to school," she offered.

Mrs. Prescott nodded gratefully. "If she asks, tell her I'll call the home in a little while. She reminded me two or three times while I was getting her up this morning."

Aunt Margaret was staring out the window when Sarah entered the bedroom. She hadn't been any hungrier than the rest of the Prescotts; her breakfast was untouched.

Sarah knelt beside the wheelchair. "I have an idea, Aunt Margaret," she whispered. "I thought of it last night when I couldn't sleep. Maybe if I take Jack Morris's painting out of the house, he'll go away. Maybe the painting is a kind of—" she hesitated "—a kind of *window* for him to come through. If we get rid of it, he won't have any connection with this house, will he?"

"The painting has changed then, just as I thought." It was a statement, not a question.

"Lots," Sarah said. "It's gotten sort of dark, and last night for just a minute I thought I saw a person in it."

Aunt Margaret didn't ask what the person looked like.

"I think you *should* get rid of it," she said slowly. "If you can do it without your mother and father asking a lot of questions. I don't think you should have anything here that belonged to him."

"And then maybe he'll go away," Sarah said eagerly. "You can stay. . ."

Aunt Margaret shook her head. "I'm not going to take that chance," she said. "You and your parents and Lloyd are my family, Sarah. It may surprise you to find out that this cranky old lady loves you. If I stay, you could all be in danger. I don't want that on my conscience."

Love. The word was like a spotlight, chasing away shadows and confusion. Sarah felt tears welling up.

"We love you, too," she said breathlessly. "And we don't want you to go." She gave Aunt Margaret a hug, then stepped back, embarrassed.

The kitchen door slammed; Lloyd was on his way to school. Sarah could hear her mother going down the basement stairs.

"You'll be late for school," Aunt Margaret scolded. "That's a bad habit to get into." She turned back to the window with its view of gray December sky and barren branches. She looked as if she, too, were crying.

Sarah darted across the hall to her parents' bedroom. Her father would be sleeping, but she was pretty sure she could slip in without waking him. The painting was in the closet where she'd left it. A quick glance told her that the scene was very dark, with no sign of the bearded man. *But I did see him last night,* she told herself. *I did see Jack Morris.*

She picked up the painting and tiptoed across the room, closing the door softly behind her. When she was sure her mother was still in the basement, she hurried downstairs to the back door and out across the snow-covered yard.

The garbage cans were behind the garage. Sarah looked up and down the alley to make sure no one was watching, then slid the painting between the cans and the garage wall. The garbage truck would make its regular pickup tomorrow afternoon, and the painting would be gone.

"You can tell *me,*" Lutie coaxed on the way to the cafeteria at noon. "The ghost came back, didn't it, Sarah? I can tell by your face. What happened?"

Sarah hesitated. Lutie would love the story about Anne Morris and her father, but Sarah had made up her mind not to talk about ghosts anymore. Besides, the terror she'd felt last night was still too fresh in her mind to permit talking about it. An adventure with a ghost might be thrilling—at least Lutie thought so—but Aunt Margaret in her wheelchair teetering at the top of the stairs was horrible.

"The window shade flew up and scared us."

She could bear to say that much. "Aunt Margaret's fed up, I guess. She's going to move back to the nursing home."

Lutie's big brown eyes widened. "You mean she's so scared she doesn't want to live with you anymore?"

"I mean she wants to move," Sarah said shortly. "She says she's making too much work for my mother."

"But that's wonderful, Sarah!" Lutie exclaimed. "You'll get your beautiful bedroom back. And we can sleep in front of the fireplace, and we can all hear the ghost tapping and listen for footsteps and singing. I wouldn't be scared if we were all there together, would you?"

"I'd rather just forget about ghosts," Sarah said. She knew she sounded irritable, but she couldn't help it.

"There's Megan." Lutie darted ahead. "I wonder what she got on the math test."

Grateful for the change of subject, Sarah followed, but more slowly. Math scores didn't seem very important that day.

When she got home from school, her mother was sitting at the kitchen table proofreading a manuscript. "Aunt Margaret goes back Saturday afternoon," she said at once, not waiting for Sarah to ask. "I hoped they wouldn't have a room available for a while, but no such luck."

Sarah took a Coke from the refrigerator and sat down opposite her mother. "You don't have to go out tonight, do you?" She tried to ask the all-important question in an offhand way.

"Not that I know of." Mrs. Prescott frowned. "Did you hear what I said about Aunt Margaret?"

Sarah nodded. "I'm sorry."

"So am I," Mrs. Prescott said. "There's no way I can convince her of it, but I've *liked* having someone to take care of these last few weeks. There've been difficult days, but most of the time I've enjoyed it. You and Lloyd are getting so grown up, you don't need to be taken care of anymore. I miss it." She sighed. "Well, we'll just have to make today and tomorrow as pleasant as possible for her. Maybe she'll change her mind again. . . ."

She won't, Sarah thought. Her mother believed Aunt Margaret was leaving because she didn't like living with the Prescotts, but Sarah knew the truth. Aunt Margaret was going because she loved her family too much to stay.

When Sarah went upstairs a few minutes later, carrying her Coke, Aunt Margaret was sitting up in bed, her eyes on the television screen. She switched off the program as Sarah came in.

"You drink too much soda," she said. "All children do, nowadays. Did your mother tell you I'm going to get back my old room at Menlo Manor? Isn't that splendid? It's a corner room— so nice and bright." Her voice was cheerful, but there were shadows under her eyes, and her little face seemed more wrinkled than usual.

"I took Jack Morris's painting out to the alley this morning," Sarah said. "You don't have to worry about it any more."

Aunt Margaret's chin lifted at the mention of Jack Morris's name. "What makes me furious is letting that—that fiend win!" She exclaimed. "I've been a fighter all my life, but I don't know how to fight this. It's difficult for me even to believe it's happening."

"Maybe with the painting gone, he won't come back," Sarah suggested again. "Maybe you should stay a while longer to see what happens."

For a moment Aunt Margaret appeared to be thinking it over. Then, "I *know* what will happen," she snapped. "And so do you. That man's hatred has lived on for more than seventy years. When I'm in this house I'm within his reach. He hates you, too, apparently—I suppose because you're alive and his daughter isn't. We're both in danger as long as I stay here. Next time Lloyd might not come home at just the right moment."

Sarah sat on the edge of the bed and finished her Coke. "Do you want to play Chinese checkers?"

The crooked little smile appeared unexpectedly. "That's your answer for everything," she said. "Well, do your homework first, and then we'll play a game or two. I understand your mother's going to be home all evening," she added. "It's a good thing. She needs the rest."

"And tomorrow is Dad's day off, so we'll all be home together."

"All day and in the evening, too," Aunt Margaret said. "That will be pleasant."

We're like spies speaking in code, Sarah thought, *telling each other everything's going to be okay, and hoping it's true.*

Seventeen

FRIDAY AFTERNOON Aunt Margaret listened to a symphony concert on the radio while Sarah, dismissed early from school, helped her mother clean house. Listening to classical music was like a little vacation, Aunt Margaret said. It didn't matter how difficult the week had been, a concert made her forget her troubles for a while.

"Can you say that about those—those *rock* people you told me about?" the old lady demanded. "What was that peculiar name?"

Sarah grinned. "The Cavemen, Aunt Margaret. And you can't compare classical music and rock. They aren't anything alike."

"I should think not," Aunt Margaret said tartly. "If you're going to use that vacuum cleaner, please close the door."

Sarah nodded and tiptoed out. She would finish the upstairs cleaning as quickly as possible, so

Aunt Margaret wouldn't have time to get lonely behind the closed door.

She was grateful, herself, for the sounds that filled the house—the music from Aunt Margaret's room, the banging of the back door as Lloyd went in and out with his friends, the distant thump of her father's hammer in the basement. She wanted those familiar sounds around her because the house—her wonderful house—felt different today. *As if something is waiting,* she thought with a shudder. *Waiting to get at us if it can.*

As she dusted dressers and polished them with lemon oil she thought of kings in their castles and pioneers at the windows of their lonely cabins. *We're standing guard against our enemy just the way they did,* she thought. The difference was that with the exception of Aunt Margaret, her family didn't know the enemy was there.

When the house was shining, Sarah helped her mother fix a dainty tray, and together they went upstairs to Aunt Margaret's room for an impromptu tea party. Mr. Prescott came in to light a fire, and eventually Lloyd appeared, too.

"What kind of sandwiches are those?"

His mother held out the plate. "Cream cheese and cucumber," she said. "You may have *one.*"

"No peanut butter? I guess I'm not hungry."

"Boys haven't changed much since my teaching days," Aunt Margaret commented, as he wandered back downstairs. "But there's something very nice about having a young boy around," she added wistfully. "So full of life. A boy like that keeps everybody young."

Mrs. Prescott poured tea into the thin china cups. "It's been good for the children to have you here, too, Aunt Margaret," she said gently. "You make all our lives more interesting. Don't you think you could—"

"No, I don't." Aunt Margaret sounded annoyed, but her lips were trembling. "I've made my decision, and I know someday I'll be sorry if I don't go. So please pass the sandwiches, and let's talk about something else."

Someday you'll be sorry. Sarah knew her great aunt was still hearing the words Jack Morris had shouted at her and her family. After all these years she continued to blame herself for being selfish. She wasn't going to be made to feel guilty again.

Dinner that evening was special, roast chicken and dressing in honor of Mr. Prescott's first meal with the family in over a week. He offered to bring Aunt Margaret downstairs in her wheelchair, but she refused the invitation.

"I'm too tired," she said. "I'd rather eat in bed." The words were blunt, but Sarah heard the message behind them. *It's hard enough leaving all of you. Let's not make it any harder.*

Only Lloyd ate his chicken and mashed potatoes with real enjoyment. Sarah listened to her parents discuss the move to Menlo Manor tomorrow, but she kept thinking about Jack Morris. Aunt Margaret's story had made him frighteningly real.

"What in the world is the matter with you, Sarah?" Mrs. Prescott demanded. "You keep peering over your shoulder in that odd way. I certainly hope you're not hearing noises again." She put her fingers to her lips the minute the words were out, but it was too late. Mr. Prescott looked up from his plate.

"What noises?" he asked. "What are you talking about?"

"Sarah hears tapping noises in the walls," Lloyd explained, eager to talk about the forbidden subject. "She thinks it's a ghost. And she hears—"

"Oh, for goodness' sake, stop!" Mrs. Prescott ordered. "We've had enough of that nonsense."

Mr. Prescott chuckled. "There's nothing ghostly about tapping in the walls at this time of the year," he said. "A squirrel can usually find a way into an old house like this one when he wants to get out of the winter wind. I'll check the attic tomorrow, and see if I can find any holes."

After dinner Sarah washed the dishes and Lloyd wiped them, complaining all the while because he couldn't go to his best friend's house to play a new video game.

"It would take just five minutes to drive me over there," he grumbled, but Mrs. Prescott shook her head.

"There's no reason why you have to go out the one evening your father's at home. Watch the basketball game with him. Try a little togetherness."

"I hate basketball," Lloyd muttered, but he sounded as if he were giving up. Sarah breathed a sigh of relief. Tonight of all nights, she wanted everyone to stay home.

As soon as the dishes were put away, she went upstairs with Gabe at her heels. Aunt Margaret was sitting up in bed, her eyes fixed on the door.

"They're not going out, are they? They mustn't."

Sarah curled up at the foot of the bed. "We're all staying home this evening," she said reassuringly. "It's going to be okay, Aunt Margaret."

"I suppose you're too busy to sit here with me for a while."

Once again Sarah had that satisfying feeling of being part of the grown-up world. Aunt Margaret needed her, wanted her close by. She brought the checkers board and arranged the marbles, trying to act relaxed even though her shoulders ached with tension.

"Take deep breaths," Aunt Margaret said abruptly. "It helps."

The game went slowly, with frequent stops for Sarah to rescue the marbles that slipped through Aunt Margaret's arthritic fingers. Or was it the temperature in the room, rather than arthritis, that made those fingers awkward? Sarah tried to tell herself that it could not be getting colder, not tonight with the whole family at home. She must be imagining it.

She was halfway under the bed, searching for a wayward marble, when her father came upstairs.

"Checking for dust, Sarah?" he inquired cheerfully. "I thought you cleaned this afternoon."

"She did," Aunt Margaret said. "She's just being patient with a clumsy old lady."

"Ruth thought you girls might like some more wood on the fire. How about it?" Without waiting for a reply, he set about adding kindling and a fresh log to the glowing ashes in the fireplace.

"That's very thoughtful of you, Davey. It does seem a little chilly in here." The words were innocent, but the quick glance Aunt Margaret sent in Sarah's direction was not. The drop in temperature was *not* Sarah's imagination.

"Why don't you stay and play checkers with us?" Sarah suggested eagerly. "Aunt Margaret's the champ—you can play her."

Mr. Prescott stirred the embers with the poker. "Thanks, but I have a basketball game to watch. It's just my good luck that the biggest game so far is being played on my night off." He rocked back on his heels and watched with satisfaction as the kindling flared. "This'll warm you up in no time."

"You're welcome to watch the game on my

television," Aunt Margaret said. The pleading in her voice was obvious to Sarah, but she didn't think her father would hear it. He'd assume Aunt Margaret was just being polite.

"Thanks, but I'll just stretch out on the couch in the living room. The screen is a lot bigger down there. You girls have fun." He started toward the door, then hesitated. "I wish you'd reconsider leaving, Aunt Margaret."

"Not that again." The old lady studied the game board. "It just won't do, Davey. I've made up my mind, so let's not discuss it anymore."

"Right." Mr. Prescott backed off, puzzled and regretful. "I'll see you later then." He stopped again at the door and turned to Sarah who had been trying desperately to think of a way to keep him upstairs. "I meant to ask at dinner, did you put that painting out with the rubbish?"

Sarah nodded, suddenly unable to speak.

"Well, don't do anything like that again without asking your mother or me." He shook a finger at her. "You and Aunt Margaret may not think much of it, but I like it. I may even hang it in the living room some day."

Aunt Margaret gasped.

"I brought it back in and put it up in the attic. That's where it's to stay until we decide what to do with it. Understood?" He smiled to show he wasn't really angry, then turned and clattered down the stairs.

"Sarah, the shepherd!"

Sarah hurtled across the room and caught the figurine as it slid over the edge of the dresser. Then she ran out to the hall, with Gabe right behind her.

"Dad, ask Mom if she wants to play checkers. Aunt Margaret's tired of playing with me all the time."

Mr. Prescott saluted from the foot of the stairs. "Will do. As soon as she gets back."

"Gets back?" Sarah reached for the bannister, fighting a wave of dizziness. "Isn't she here?"

"She took Lloyd over to Teddy's house. He kept begging, so I told him to go. He'd have been bored stiff watching the game with me." There was a roar from the television set in the living room. "I'll tell Mom as soon as she comes in. She won't be gone long."

"Sarah!"

As Sarah turned back to the bedroom, a window shade flew up with a firecracker-snap. Aunt Margaret had pulled the comforter to her chin and was peering over it with the panicky eyes of a child. "Look at the rocker!"

The chair, halfway between the bed and the fireplace, was rocking gently. *As if someone just got up,* Sarah thought. *No—as if someone is sitting in it now!*

Gabe began to whimper.

"Come over here," Aunt Margaret pleaded. "Sit on the bed close to me."

The chair rocked faster. "I'd better call Dad," Sarah said. "He'll see for himself—"

"He won't see a thing! Nothing will happen if he's here, you know that. He'll just think I'm a silly old woman and you're a naughty girl with an overactive imagination."

Sarah went back to the bed and sank down. She couldn't take her eyes off the chair.

"Give me the shepherd," Aunt Margaret whispered. "He knows how much I value it. He'll break it if he can."

No need to ask who *he* was. Aunt Margaret slid the figurine under the comforter and pressed the covers around it. Sarah felt as if she were trapped in a nightmare.

Far away, in the safe downstairs world, the telephone rang. She heard her father's heavy step, then his voice, gruff at the interruption.

A pill bottle flew off the table and rolled across the carpet.

"Sarah." Mr. Prescott was at the foot of the stairs again. The rocking chair slowed. "Sarah, your mother stopped to buy milk at the supermarket, and now she can't get the car started. I'm going to have to walk over there and see if I can get it going."

"No!" Sarah shouted. "You mustn't!"

"Of course 1 must." Her father sounded disgusted. "Don't think 1 wouldn't rather stay home."

"He can't let Ruth sit there in the cold!" Aunt Margaret exclaimed. "Don't argue, Sarah."

"But we'll be alone!" The words came out in a wail, cut short by the slamming of the front door.

"We *are* alone," Aunt Margaret said. "It's too late, Sarah. We'll just have to face whatever comes."

The rocking chair began to move again. Gabe, who had been crouched close to the bed, gave a whimper of protest, scrambled to his feet, and raced downstairs.

Eighteen

Sмакт DOG," Aunt Margaret gritted the words. "I think you'd better go too, Sarah. Get out of the house. Something dreadful is going to happen."

The chair was moving faster now, rocking so far back that it came close to tipping. Behind it, the fireplace logs flared and sent up showers of sparks.

Sarah gripped Aunt Margaret's hand and tried to decide what to do. She could call the Martins next door, or she could call the police again and tell them . . . tell them what? *The chair in my great-aunt's bedroom won't stop rocking?* Impossible! Anyway, the telephone was downstairs. She didn't dare leave Aunt Margaret even for a minute.

"I mean it, Sarah. I want you to go. Please!"

An invisible hand swept along the mantel, scattering photos and the vase of artificial flowers.

Aunt Margaret gave a little shriek and covered her eyes.

"He's here," she gasped. "I can feel him in this room. That evil man—"

The bed moved joltingly. This time it was Sarah who cried out. She leapt backward, away from the bed, and was almost to the door before she could stop herself. When she looked back, Aunt Margaret appeared to have fainted. Her hands had fallen away from her face, and her eyes were closed. Her skin was gray against the white pillowcase.

The bed moved again, a little sidewise hop, as if something monstrous were under it and trying to escape. The lamp flickered. Sarah ran to the dresser and fumbled through the top drawer, looking for the flashlight she'd stored there. She found it just as the lamp blinked once more and went out with a *pop*. Except for the glow of the fire, the room was dark.

Sarah stood frozen, the flashlight clutched in her trembling hands. Its beam made a thin tunnel of light that danced around her feet. She could hear the rocking chair creaking in the dark. *Run!* it seemed to say. *You'll be sorry if you don't.*

She took a deep breath and pointed the flashlight toward the rocker. A tall man was sitting there, red-haired and bearded, with a wolfish grin that was more terrifying than a scowl. As she stared, not believing, he raised one hand in a mock hello, then gestured casually toward the fireplace. The firescreen tumbled forward with a crash, and a flaming log rolled out on the carpet. Bits of burning bark scattered around it, and the carpet began to smolder.

"No!" Sarah screamed. "Don't!"

The bearded figure smiled its hideous smile and gestured again. Another burning log hurtled out of the fireplace. Sick with horror, Sarah saw the circle of burning carpet widen. She knew what Jack Morris wanted to do. He wanted to start a fire, here in Aunt Margaret's room, like the one that had killed his daughter many years ago. He was going to sit there, rocking and smiling, while the whole house went up in flames.

The terror that till now had kept Sarah from moving was swept away in a surge of anger. She dashed to the bed and snatched up the blanket that lay folded at Aunt Margaret's feet. *Smother a fire . . .* that was what she'd learned in first-aid class at school. *A fire needs oxygen to burn. . . .* She threw the blanket over the burning logs and stamped it down.

Behind her, the bearded man laughed. It was the ugliest sound Sarah had ever heard. She swung the flashlight toward the rocking chair in time to see the ghostly figure raise its hand a third time. Flames burst through the center of the blanket.

Frantic, Sarah scooped up the small rug in front

of the dresser and threw it on top of the blanket.
If that didn't stop the fire, she'd have to drag Aunt
Margaret out of bed, lift her into her wheelchair,
get the wheelchair down the stairs. . . .

Smoke swirled out from under the blanket, but
the flames disappeared beneath the heavy rug.
Sarah turned back to Jack Morris. He was no
longer smiling. His expression was a curious
blend of sorrow and fear, and he was looking at
something behind Sarah.

Sarah whirled and discovered a slim girl in a
blue dress standing near the doorway. The girl's
light brown hair fell loosely to her shoulders, and
her eyes were wide and intense. She walked into
the flashlight's beam without seeming to notice
Sarah. All her attention was focused on the man
in the rocking chair.

"I've come to stop you," she said in a low voice
edged with pain. "You're doing something bad.
Always something bad."

The bearded man started to get up, then sank
back. "Go away," he snarled. "Don't interfere.
It's *her* fault you're dead." He gestured toward
the bed.

The girl shook her head. "Margaret's my
friend," she said. "I've come to take care of her."
She turned and looked at Sarah for the first time.
"*We'll* take care of her," she said. "Sarah and
I."

The girl's voice was so soft that Sarah had to

strain to hear, but there was no mistaking the power behind it. She remembered what Aunt Margaret had said about her friend Anne. *She was a frail-looking girl, but she never backed down. . . .*

The ghost of Jack Morris glared up at his daughter. Sarah trembled at the fury in those eyes, but Anne didn't move, even when the man's big hands curled into fists.

"I was doing it for you," he growled. "You should be grateful."

"You were doing it for yourself," Anne said in the same small, cool voice. "You want to blame Margaret for what you brought on yourself. But now you are going to stop."

They stared at each other, and Sarah held her breath. She could feel the battle that raged between father and daughter, but she could do nothing. Aunt Margaret's life, and maybe her own, depended on who won, and all she could do was watch.

And then there was a sound, a long, drawn-out sigh, almost a groan. Slowly, the figure of the red-bearded man began to change. The furious glare faded, and the hard lines of the man's face softened and grew less distinct. The big body seemed to waver in the circle of light; it grew fainter, then stronger, then faint again, until at last it was gone.

The rocking chair was empty.

Anne Morris walked over to the bed. "When she wakes up, tell her gentle Annie loves her." She smiled down at Aunt Margaret's small, wrinkled face. "Tell her she mustn't be sorry anymore."

And then she, too, was gone.

Nineteen

SARAH SAT DOWN HARD on the floor. She hugged herself and took long, shuddering breaths. After a moment the bedside lamp flicked on, and the air began to warm, but still she sat there. She wasn't sure her legs would hold her if she tried to stand up.

Downstairs, Gabe was growling fiercely, the growls punctuated by anxious barks. Sarah guessed he must have been doing that ever since he ran away, but she hadn't heard him until now.

At last she scrambled to her feet and touched Aunt Margaret's cold hand.

"Are you okay?"

She thought the thin fingers returned her squeeze, but she couldn't be sure.

"Aunt Margaret, Jack Morris is gone! For good, I think. Anne sent him away."

This time the pressure was unmistakable.

"Shall I call your doctor?"

The blue eyes flew open. "Don't you dare. I'm resting." The eyes closed again.

Sarah tucked her great-aunt's hand under the covers and looked around. The bedroom was a mess. She began picking up the scattered photographs and pill bottles and straightened the portrait over the fireplace. The shepherd figurine was still under the comforter; she took it out and put it back in its usual place on the dresser.

There was nothing to be done about the badly burned carpet and the scorched blanket and rug. Maybe tomorrow she could find another little rug in the attic—one big enough to hide the burned spot. It would look peculiar, dropped in the center of the carpet, but that didn't matter.

Nothing mattered as long as Jack Morris was gone.

Thinking about the attic reminded her that the painting was still there. She picked up the flashlight and went out into the hall. Gabe was halfway up the stairs, still growling. When he saw her, he hurried the rest of the way and licked her hand.

"Chicken dog!"

Together they climbed the attic stairs, Sarah much reassured by the dog's willingness to go along. "There's a light switch up here somewhere," she told him. "If it doesn't work—we'll run."

It worked. The cluttered attic spread out around

them, a jumble of old furniture, crates, and trunks. The painting was balanced against a box in plain view.

It was beautiful. The ominous shadows were gone, and there was no figure lurking among the trees. Sarah stood at the top of the stairs and looked across at the glowing greens, the bright shafts of sunlight. She didn't want to get any closer—not yet—but she knew now why she'd liked the painting so much the first time she saw it.

When they went back downstairs, Aunt Margaret's eyes were open. She looked pale and exhausted, but her voice was firm.

"I want to know exactly what happened," she said. "All of it—after the bed started jumping around. I think I must have had a little fainting spell about then."

Sarah nodded. She passed quickly over the ghost of Jack Morris; maybe she would be able to talk about him someday, but the memory was still too frightening to bear thinking about. The ghost of Anne Morris was very different.

"She stood right here where I'm standing, Aunt Margaret. And she said to tell you gentle Annie loves you very much and doesn't want you to be sorry anymore."

"You actually saw her then." Aunt Margaret sighed. "How did she look?"

"She was pretty. And she was brave! It was *so*

scary, the way she stood up to her father and told him he had to stop frightening you."

"I'd say Sarah Prescott was just as brave as Anne Morris," Aunt Margaret said unexpectedly. "If it weren't for you, this house would have burned down, just the way he planned it—and I'd be gone, too. I thank you for that."

"I was scared stiff," Sarah said. "I wanted to run away."

Aunt Margaret raised her eyebrows. "Well, of course you were scared," she snapped. "If you weren't scared, being brave wouldn't mean a thing. Now, what are you going to tell your parents?"

"I-I don't know."

"You and I understand what happened here tonight, but I can't imagine being able to make your mother and father believe it. Particularly your mother." Aunt Margaret frowned. "Here's what I'm going to tell them. I'll just say a log rolled out of the fireplace, and you courageously put out the fire. What are *you* going to say?"

Sarah didn't know how to answer, so Aunt Margaret continued.

"I think I shall say it gives me a great deal of comfort to see what a responsible young woman you've become, and I've decided I won't go back to Menlo Manor, for a while, at least. After all, if Jack Morris is gone, there's no reason for me to leave, is there? Unless you think I really do make too much work for your mother. Please tell me the truth."

It was the first time a grown-up had asked Sarah's advice. "Mom says she likes having someone to take care of," she said carefully. "She really wants you to stay. We all do."

Aunt Margaret looked at her with a thoughtful expression. "If I left, you could have your bedroom back," she said. "Don't pretend you wouldn't like that."

Sarah looked around at the room and let herself remember just how much she'd enjoyed having it all to herself. She wanted to be completely honest.

"I do love this room," she said finally, "but it doesn't matter as much as I thought it did. I want you to stay. It's really nice having you be part of our family."

They sat in silence for a while, and then Aunt Margaret sighed again and reached for the television control. A blast of sound leapt from the set, and five young men, singing and playing guitars, drums, and keyboard, appeared in bursts of colored light.

"Good heavens, what a racket!" Aunt Margaret fingered the control, and the young men disappeared. "Who on earth were those wild-looking monsters?"

Sarah didn't know whether to laugh or be insulted. "Those were the Cavemen, Aunt Margaret," she said. "And they're not monsters! They're just the best rock group in the world, that's all. I was going to go to their concert next month but—" She stopped. It was one more thing that didn't seem quite as important as it had before. Before tonight.

"Well, pardon me all to pieces." A picture of a family of ducklings appeared, then a game show contestant clasping his hands over his head, then the singers once more. "If they're the best in the world, I suppose we ought to give them a chance," she said, and settled into her pillows with a look of real pain.

"You don't have to do that," Sarah said. "I can go downstairs to listen—at least until someone gets home."

Aunt Margaret shook her head. "No need. I'll live through it. I've lived through worse." Her mouth lifted in a crooked smile. "But not *much* worse," she added, and closed her eyes again, in case Sarah intended to argue.

About the Author

BETTY REN WRIGHT is the author of numerous award-winning books for young readers, including *Christina's Ghost* and *Ghosts Beneath Our Feet,* which were both IRA-CBC Children's Choices, and *The Dollhouse Murders,* which was a *Booklist* Reviewer's Choice and a nominee for the Mystery Writers of America's Edgar Allan Poe Award.

Ms. Wright says of *A Ghost in the House,* "I've been around elderly people a great deal. Their lives, and their children's lives, are so much richer when they share time and experiences."

Ms. Wright lives in Wisconsin with her husband, George Frederickson, who is an artist.

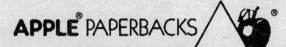

APPLE® PAPERBACKS

Pick an Apple and Polish Off Some Great Reading!

BEST-SELLING APPLE TITLES

☐ MT43944-8	**Afternoon of the Elves** Janet Taylor Lisle	**$2.75**
☐ MT43109-9	**Boys Are Yucko** Anna Grossnickle Hines	**$2.75**
☐ MT43473-X	**The Broccoli Tapes** Jan Slepian	**$2.95**
☐ MT42709-1	**Christina's Ghost** Betty Ren Wright	**$2.75**
☐ MT43461-6	**The Dollhouse Murders** Betty Ren Wright	**$2.75**
☐ MT43444-6	**Ghosts Beneath Our Feet** Betty Ren Wright	**$2.75**
☐ MT44351-8	**Help! I'm a Prisoner in the Library** Eth Clifford	**$2.75**
☐ MT44567-7	**Leah's Song** Eth Clifford	**$2.75**
☐ MT43618-X	**Me and Katie (The Pest)** Ann M. Martin	**$2.75**
☐ MT41529-8	**My Sister, The Creep** Candice F. Ransom	**$2.75**
☐ MT42883-7	**Sixth Grade Can Really Kill You** Barthe DeClements	**$2.75**
☐ MT40409-1	**Sixth Grade Secrets** Louis Sachar	**$2.75**
☐ MT42882-9	**Sixth Grade Sleepover** Eve Bunting	**$2.75**
☐ MT41732-0	**Too Many Murphys** Colleen O'Shaughnessy McKenna	**$2.75**

Available wherever you buy books, or use this order form.

Scholastic Inc., P.O. Box 7502, 2931 East McCarty Street, Jefferson City, MO 65102

Please send me the books I have checked above. I am enclosing $_____ (please add $2.00 to cover shipping and handling). Send check or money order — no cash or C.O.D.s please.

Name _____

Address _____

City _____ **State/Zip** _____

Please allow four to six weeks for delivery. Offer good in the U.S.A. only. Sorry, mail orders are not available to residents of Canada. Prices subject to change.

APP591